INTO THE STARS

Michael Blake

ZOVA BOOKS
LOS ANGELES

ZOVA BOOKS

This book is a work of fiction. References to real people, events, establishments, organizations, or locales are intended only to provide a sense of authenticity and are used fictitiously. All other characters, and all incidents and dialogue are drawn from the author's imagination and are not to be construed as real.

First ZOVA Books edition 2011.

INTO THE STARS. Copyright © 2011 by Michael Blake.

All rights reserved.

Printed in the United States of America.

No part of this book may be used or reproduced in any manner whatsoever without written permission except in the case of brief quotations embodied in critical articles and reviews.

For information or permission contact:

ZOVA Books
P.O. Box 21833, Long Beach, California 90801
www.zovabooks.com

ISBN-13: 978-0615510538
ISBN-10: 0615510531

Cover Design ©Daniel Pearson

Like all other words on paper, *Into the Stars* did not come out of requests, payment or a desire for success. It came out of my heart and soul.

— *Michael Lennox Blake*

THE HOLE

The bomb crater was a large one, large enough to shelter a dozen men. The big hole held seven people. Six of them had no need of shelter. They had been dead for hours. The seventh man was still alive. He sat against the sloping wall of the crater, his arms folded over his knees, his forehead resting on his arms as if he had fallen asleep. He was coated with grime and sweat, and though he showed no sign of injury, the picture he presented was of overwhelming defeat.

His name was Ledyard Dixon, and despite being unwounded, a glance at his surroundings gave the impression that he too would soon be dead. A dismal, gray rain, steady and unforgiving, was falling. Gentle as the downfall was, it seemed unnecessary and cruel in its soaking of the poor men strewn about the crater, as if they were discarded toys left to rust. The man left alive was just as impervious to the moisture falling all about him.

Some of the dead were missing limbs or chunks of torso, torn off earlier in the day by shrapnel. One body had pitched forward and rested on headless shoulders halfway down the incline. Its head lay a few feet away, poised at the lip of a fetid pool of water which contained bits of miscellaneous trash, empty ration cans, a human leg, excrement and other unidentifiable remains of carnage.

Ledyard did not bother to look up as an artillery shell whistled overhead and impacted close by, near enough to splatter his already saturated uniform with drops of mud. He moved slightly as the mud shower hit but he did not flinch, not even when the artillery barrage intensified.

Ledyard was struggling to reconnect his mind, a mind shattered into pieces by the horror of his circumstances. Though he barely moved, the young soldier struggled mightily to create patterns of thought that could again be processed. Instinctively, he knew he must leave the crater, but for hours he had not been able to trust his motor functions. If he was ever to move he had to regain thought, and he was trying to dream himself back to life.

A sudden gust of rain-driven wind swept over the edge of the crater and kissed Ledyard's cheeks. Just as suddenly, he could feel the breeze on Lake Michigan as his little sloop knifed across the water. He was at the tiller and a girl's full, cool lips brushed against his jaw as they moved up to his mouth.

A brief sensation of warmth passed through Ledyard's inert body. Lifting his head slightly, he opened his eyes.

Below him, he saw the pool of water that had collected at the bottom of the crater, its surface marbled with streaks of urine, blood and fuel. He closed his eyes again and saw a brush in his Uncle Cecil's hand expertly daubing red watercolor on heavy paper mounted on an easel. He saw himself seated cross-legged on the floor of his uncle's summer studio, gazing up in awe as Cecil, using only the quick strokes of his hand, created the blurred image of a freight train rushing out of a curve.

He heard his mother call and turned to see her framed in the studio doorway on a chestnut horse, its flanks heaving from a recent gallop. Sweat was dripping from the horse's belly and there were drops running down the temples of her beautiful face.

The lemonade pitcher was sweating too. It stood on a long table in front of his uncle's studio. Surrounding it were wedges of watermelon and cold cuts and fresh bread and condiments, great bowls of potato salad and dishes of sweet berries. Everything was resting like a still life portrait in summer shade.

At the far end of the table sat Grandpa Clarkson with his cigar, distinguished in a tweed vest and white shirt, patting the heads of children who came to pay homage to him and his trademark: a sack of candy and small coins sitting near the edge of the table.

The adults sat and smoked, telling long, funny stories while the ice in their highball glasses melted and the children played. Ledyard often joined in the games but just as often he was content to sit in an empty space at the far end of the table, letting the secure hum of happy voices carry him while he arranged his collection of metal horses and men.

The arrival of his father, signaled by the distant chug of an automobile engine, brought Ledyard and the other children out onto the vehicle's running boards. His father grinned behind the wheel as if he were steering a marvelous float.

Ledyard never minded sharing his father's attention, for he did not know him very well nor did he yearn for a closer bond. His family was considered progressive for its time, demanding from its members only the basic rules of conduct. Ledyard was allowed to do what he pleased and grew up free of the responsibility to love. In his eyes, father and mother were simply "them," the radiant pair to whom he belonged.

As the afternoon feast wore on, Ledyard slipped from his chair and stretched out under the table, watching the shifting legs of adults and hazily contemplating the fringes of the checkered tablecloth as it furled and unfurled with every shift of the incoming breeze.

He saw the sail over the shoulder of his lover, it too flapping languidly in a summer's breeze. Her palm was pressed against the bare skin of his chest and her lips were tapping out an unhurried cadence against his, speaking the mysterious language of first love.

Ledyard opened his eyes again and discovered that the battlefield was cloaked in darkness. He also found that he could move. Squirming to one side and using his fingers like claws on the slick-walled crater, he crept to the top.

The thunder of artillery boomed from near and far, but there was nothing to see in the flashes. Ledyard squinted into the blackness around him, hoping that some landmark might appear from which he could get bearings. But nothing was revealed, and after a few minutes of futile staring he began to feel tired.

He let himself slip away from the edge of the crater and slid inch-by-inch back to his original position along the slimy wall. He nestled the side of his face against the mud, made his hands into a pillow and tried for sleep by silently repeating:

"Now I lay me down to sleep. I pray the Lord my soul to keep. If I die before I wake, I pray the Lord my soul to take."

But Ledyard could not keep other thoughts from intruding. Perhaps it was necessary in the process of rebuilding cohesion of thought. Images of the trench and what had brought him to the crater played in his mind. Somewhere in the reconstruction of recent events, he lost consciousness and slept.

THE TRENCH

The trench was different from the others. It was not fused to the vast maze of earthen cuts that comprised the allied lines. It was a forward observation post, far in front of the primary fortifications, a place which afforded a close-up view of the enemy and the long strip of no-man's land in between.

The men who made it home called it the trench with a million dollar view, because it had cost so much to decimate the land that lay before it. As far as the eye could see, the land was flat and barren, broken occasionally by the shattered, burned and denuded remains of a tree, planted like a broken matchstick in a desert of muck.

On the horizon what looked like long, spiraling lines of brush could be discerned. The brush was actually barbed wire, taller than a man and strung out for miles in front of the enemy's own miserable trenches.

He had come to the trench as part of the first great infusion of American blood, and though he'd had only cursory training, his arrival as part of a great force was greeted with exuberant relief. The Frenchmen Ledyard and his fellow Americans supplanted seemed to have been made small by years of warfare. They were sullen and dirty and, while they were happy to see Americans at the front, there was little light in their eyes.

Ledyard knew most of the boys in his company, for they had all gone through boot camp together. They were the typical American blend of northeastern Irish-Catholic, Baptists from the south, Lutherans, Episcopalians and Methodists from the Midwest. There were boys from the backwoods who hardly knew how to bathe, sons of steelworkers who conducted life by rote, fast boys from the big city and a smattering of young men like himself who had grown up in Arrow shirts and knew something of the wider world of travel and manners, literature and privilege. All of them ended up in a trench on Belgium soil for the same avowed reason: they felt a sense of duty, not only to answer their country's call, but to help people in need.

Spirits were high during the first days they possessed the trench. Skies were clear, the sun was warm, the breeze was cool and they were reunited with the earth after pitching about for days on a crowded troop ship in the stormy Atlantic. They were active now, running wire, reinforcing parapets, laying new planking in the bottom of the trench and watching an enemy that they all knew was out there but didn't seem threatening. They had arrived during a lull in the fighting.

The lull was extended by the arrival of heavy rain which descended on them the third night and lasted nearly a week. They had heard about the rain dreaded by every veteran, but nothing could have prepared them for the onslaught from heaven. It blew and pounded and roared. It came down in unbelievable sheets that mired their world in liquid. The ditches they lived in filled up. Latrines overflowed and saturated the wet air with stink. The narrow, oozing walls of the trench collapsed again and again, revealing French and German bodies that had been hastily buried after previous battles.

The boys were pressed into service as headquarters runners, dashing back and forth with communiques. The round trip took more than an hour, and by the time a message reached the trench, some development had usually rendered it obsolete.

Ledyard and his friend Drayton seemed constantly on the run. Sometimes they paused to share a few words or a cigarette, but most often they would simply shout or wave as they ran past each other.

There had been no sign of the enemy. Their lines had been so quiet that while digging out a new latrine one evening Ledyard and Drayton had discussed the possibility that the Germans might have withdrawn entirely. This hopeful speculation was dispelled on the morning of the third day after the rain had gone.

Dawn broke bright and sunny and the company captain, an energetic New Yorker with flame red hair and round spectacles, had momentarily forgotten where he was. Eager to assess the rain damage in front of the trench, he had climbed onto one of the parapets for a look around. After a few moments of scrutinizing the fortifications a sudden urge to yawn seized him and, as his mouth rolled open, he threw his arms toward the sky in a full stretch.

This simple act drew a barrage of sniper fire from the enemy line. One of the bullets struck the captain flush on the forehead and, missing a portion of his skull, he tumbled back into the trench, dead before he hit the ground. Another captain replaced him within hours. This one was short, wiry and not inclined to yawn on parapets as he went about the business of getting his men ready to fight.

Though they knew little more than which end was which, the new commander assigned Ledyard and Drayton to a machine gun. That same morning the two young men set to work building a nest for themselves and their weapon.

They wore their soaking uniforms around the clock. There was no way to sleep or eat or smoke or talk or get warm. Weapons were useless. War was useless. Humankind was useless. There was only rain.

During this inundation Ledyard slept under a square of canvas and a few scraps of tin with Drayton. Like most of the other soldiers they clung to each other for warmth through the long, wet nights.

Drayton came from Montana and bore the classic features of a westerner. He had a sharp nose, a pinched mouth, eyes that shone like marbles and a jagged scar along his jaw from a boyhood mishap. His hands were like sandpaper and shaking with him was like pumping braided steel.

They had been bunkmates during training and despite their diverse backgrounds had formed a solid bond. Not many words had to pass between them, and when they did talk the subject invariably turned to a shared regard for horses, a topic which provided limitless discourse for the two boys.

At last the weather began to clear. Once the storm moved out the trench became a scene of perpetual activity as mud and water were cleared away, parapets were repaired, wire was restrung and walkways in the narrow trench were re-shored.

Ledyard and Drayton stuck together, performing routine duties as a team and volunteering as a team. The two friends didn't talk about it much, but the irony was obvious. Their feverish labors were being carried out to make them better able to fight and die and they acknowledged the irony with a wisecrack that was soon in common usage throughout the company.

"It's all an illuuuuusion."

Picking a random individual from their company, each guessed how long it would be before he had to urinate again, and thus it was determined that Drayton would fire and Ledyard would feed bullets into the gun.

Enemy sniper fire continued sporadically, but about mid-afternoon a palpable quiet settled over the battlefield and word was passed that an enemy attack was imminent. Standing side by side, the men gripped their rifles, watched the battlefield as openly as they dared, and waited.

The attack was signaled by the distant boom of a big gun and the shrill, dying whine of an incoming shell as it flew overhead and exploded the earth as it impacted somewhere behind the forward observation trench. Before the shell exploded, there were many more distant booms, and an instant later the air was alive with bombs.

The whole of the land's crust blew up as shells came to ground. The men of Ledyard's company hugged the walls of their still-soaked trench in disbelief as an artificial rain of fire and smoke and noise poured over them. The force of one shell landing near was enough to shake a person senseless, but one was followed so quickly by another that the bombardment became a surreal monstrous cataract of sound and vibration. For more than an hour the company huddled with clenched teeth in the cut earth, enduring blast after mind-numbing blast.

One soldier ran screaming onto the field and disappeared in a maelstrom of destruction. Others broke down in tears. A few pieces of errant shrapnel found their way into the trench, maiming or killing a luckless half dozen. Most of the company hung on, as if riding out a typhoon, knowing all the while that when the shelling stopped they would be facing a greater dilemma.

Seconds after it ceased officers were calling out, "Battle stations, battle stations!" The order was seen rather than heard, for the shouted words carried into each soldier's ringing ears like distant, dreamy incantations.

Ledyard and Drayton scrambled up the steps of a ladder and dove into the sandbagged nest they had constructed atop one of the parapets. The boy from Montana plopped down behind the trigger, throwing his legs out on either side of the machine gun as Ledyard struggled to engage the cartridge belt. From the time the shelling stopped until they had situated themselves took only a few seconds, but when they glanced up for their first look at the battlefield, the enemy was already upon them.

Hundreds of armed men were advancing out of the still smoking plain in a zig-zag, curling around craters and sidestepping or hopping debris. They were firing as they came.

The two machine gunners knew nothing of war, and it was doubtful that either had ever done anything more violent than imagine taking another human life. But Ledyard tapped his partner on the head, Drayton depressed the weapon's trigger and the team began to shoot at every human figure in front of them.

The first shots went wild, but when he saw men begin to fall Drayton relaxed. In moments, he was calmly sweeping the field like an expert. Ledyard watched just as objectively as he fed the gun its bullets. Soon he was shouting over the din to his mate, telling him to aim the gun here or there. In the frenzy of battle, neither one of the friends paused to evaluate their actions. It was a simple matter of kill or be killed, and it was satisfying to see so many of the enemy tumble before their effortless fire.

A curious kind of frustration soon overtook the gunners in the nest on the parapet. No matter how many of the enemy they killed there seemed to be just as many as before. Ledyard and Drayton wondered where they could all be coming from and how many they would have to kill before they fell back.

In minutes Drayton's trigger hand was cramping and the boys frantically switched places. They had begun to receive heavy fire and must have exposed themselves while jockeying about in the nest because a bullet suddenly skidded over the crown of Ledyard's helmet. The same slug pinged off Drayton's headgear. For a moment the boys gazed at each other stupefied. When they looked up again they saw an object hurtling toward them. It was twirling lazily through smoke filled space on a course that seemed destined for a perfect hit. There was nothing the boys could do but cover their ears as they pressed their noses into the dirt, waiting for the explosion.

The grenade came to earth just in front of the nest, obliging the little wall of sandbags Ledyard and Drayton had built to take the brunt of the blast. But the concussion of the well-aimed bomb knocked them both silly.

They flopped like caught fish in a shower of sand, their brains banging around against the walls of their skulls. When they recovered their senses and sat up to look out they were amazed to see that the enemy was receding into the mists of smoke from which they had come. The two friends climbed to their feet and, like schoolboys celebrating good riddance, shook their upraised fists at the retreating foe.

COUNTER-ATTACK

There was no time for rejoicing and barely time to acknowledge the two dozen comrades who were among the dead and wounded. Once they had located the gear scattered during the attack, Ledyard and Drayton busied themselves with getting ready for the counter attack that would now take place.

As the surviving combatants did what they could to put the forward observation post back in order, fresh troops began to arrive and when the trench was fully augmented with new faces word was passed that an artillery barrage, preceding an infantry attack, would begin in precisely fifteen minutes.

Ledyard and Drayton gulped a few mouthfuls of food, drank as much water as they could hold and found a spot not far from their captain to wait out the last minutes before going over the top.

The fifteen minutes passed but there was no firing and orders were received that headquarters was postponing the counter-attack for two hours. No explanation for the delay was given and it was greeted among the rank and file with relief and jitters.

Going over the top involved a certain process that began with checking and re-checking weapons, evacuating bowels and bladders and chatting with pals before turning inward as the minutes wasted away to zero. Allowing for minor idiosyncratic deviations, the process for each soldier was the same whether they were veterans or virgins.

The fighters repeated this excruciating process once more only to see the new attack time come and go in abject silence.

Like their brothers-in-arms, Ledyard and Drayton responded to the new delay with mute exasperation and sinking hearts. It was as if they were condemned only to have the noose removed moments before the springing of the trap . . . then to have the hour of execution reset and the coils dropped over their necks again. After the second postponement everyone was grumbling.

They could not have guessed the reasons for the delays but the initiated knew full well that a snafu in procuring hot water for a general's bath was as good a candidate as any for the hang fire. And though no one talked of it openly, the hold ups gave the once reeling enemy ample time to fortify it's positions and receive reinforcements.

In the case of the troops manning the forward observation trench this is precisely what had happened, and when the artillery barrage finally began and ended, they charged out into no-man's land a full six hours after their tormentors had been repulsed. The enemy had indeed been refortified and reinforced, and was now eagerly waiting to give back what they had received earlier in the day.

Ledyard and Drayton went over together, but the ensuing chaos quickly separated them. Ledyard was watching Drayton hurdle a cluster of enemy bodies when he tripped at full speed and fell flat on his face.

Before he could pick himself up Ledyard saw several soldiers speed past him. Then he heard the whistle of an incoming shell and saw it land on those who had passed. He pressed his face against the earth as dirt, smoking shrapnel, and body parts landed all around him.

His body felt suddenly leaden as he pulled himself to his feet. Briefly, he thought of turning back. But his comrades were still running toward the enemy and, thinking that his heavy legs would lighten as he ran, Ledyard moved forward at a trot.

He could see the enemy lines clearly now. By some dubious miracle the great rolls of wire fronting the enemy trench had not been breached, making it impossible for the attackers to advance once they reached it. The foe's machine guns were busy now, mowing down the Americans in the same way Ledyard and Drayton had done. People were falling everywhere and those not being hit were going down of their own volition, seeking shelter where there was none.

As he reached the wire Ledyard dove to earth. There he lay as if pinned, expecting the hot sting of a bullet at any moment. When he chanced a look ahead, he saw the bodies of those who had tried to penetrate the wire hanging like flies in a web. He recognized the one closest to him. It was the leader of his unit, the veteran captain, and his face was frozen with a look of such intense consternation that Ledyard expected him to cry out his dismay at the botched counter-offensive. But the captain hung where he was and Ledyard buried his face in the dirt again.

From the instant he had gone over the top time had

ceased to be measurable, and Ledyard was not sure how long he lay in front of the wire. Gradually, however, he sensed that the firing had slackened. He also became aware of happy voices shouting in a foreign language and when he dared to peek up he saw many of the enemy standing in full view atop their trench calling out to the battlefield.

Twisting his head reflexively for a look behind he saw the distant figures of men staggering back to the lines from whence they had come and realized that he was now alone with the dead and wounded, a stone's throw from men who would kill him if they discovered he was alive.

Ledyard's mind raced through alternatives. He could jump up and fire at the enemy, hoping to hit one or two before he was killed. He could try to surrender. He could lay still until nightfall and try to crawl away. Knowing that if he kept breathing, possibilities for living remained, Ledyard lay still.

Ledyard did not know how much time had passed when he saw that it was growing dark. A drop of something wet splattered on his cheek, and in his disorientation Ledyard briefly thought he was bleeding. But there had been no sound and no pain.

He opened his eyes. The battlefield had grown quite dark with the arrival of low, heavy clouds. A single raindrop had struck his cheek.

The clouds moved closer to the ground and the rain increased. Ledyard watched the enemy lines grow more and more blurred as the wind blew up and drove the rain across the battlefield in waving curtains. The more it rained the more excited he became. Still he did not move. As long as the rain kept up he would not try to make a getaway. He would tough it out until dark when his chances would be even better.

The rain was still pouring as darkness enveloped the battlefield. Ledyard decided the time was right but to his surprise he found he could not move. The messages his brain was sending to the rest of his body were going undelivered. Perhaps he was merely so stiff and cold that his parts could not be stirred to life. Perhaps he had been hit and didn't know it. Perhaps he had suffered a mental breakdown rendering his motor functions inoperative.

Again and again he asked the fingers of his right hand to move, and finally, like the tentative legs of a spider, they began to lift. The feeling in his fingers traveled up his forearm, through his biceps and into his shoulder, then over his back, down his legs and into his toes. These sensations gave him confidence but confidence alone could not move the whole of his body. Its one hundred and seventy pounds was as immovable as cement. Clamping his jaws tight to suppress any involuntary groans that might carry to the ears of the enemy, Ledyard summoned all his strength and rolled onto his back.

He lay still for a few moments and let the rain pelt his upturned face. The stinging drops revived him and with greater ease he rolled onto his stomach. He waited only a few seconds until rolling again. He repeated the process and soon he was rolling blindly over the dark, swampy battlefield with the feeling of a boy scout performing some leisurely stunt.

At last he came to a stop, propped himself on his elbows, and looking around, realized he had lost all cognizance of direction. There was no way to discern where the safety of his lines lay, but even if there had been a sign twinkling in the dark he would not have gone there for fear of being mistaken for a midnight raider.

Slowly, he planted his hands in the muck, drew one of his legs under him and rose. He staggered a bit but managed to keep his feet and was on the verge of taking a step when a blinding light blossomed with a pop high above his head, turning night to day.

In a split-second he understood it was a flare and in another split second he saw the great rolls of wire standing nearby and knew that he was still within shouting distance of the enemy. He was also in range of their rifles which immediately began to crackle through the rain. A slug whizzed past one of his ears and Ledyard lurched forward on wobbly legs. He tried to zig and zag, but his legs buckled and he went down to the mud as the first flare died.

Another flare went off and again the rifles reported, but the marksmen seemed to have lost track of him for none of the bullets came close. He lay still in the ooze as the enemy wasted several more flares trying to find him.

Ledyard lay prone in the mud and found he could no longer hold back the emotions that had been hammering at him all day and night but which he had been too preoccupied to serve. They started as a trickle but quickly became a flood of exhaustion and self-pity and fear, melancholy and despair and hopelessness.

He began to cry, first in spasmodic whispers, then in an unbroken stream of full-throated unabashed sobs. For twenty minutes, the boy lay in the mud and rain of no-man's land, lost in the blackened debris of war, wailing out his agony in an unstoppable torrent of tears.

The rain had nearly stopped by the time Ledyard was finished, and though he was more exhausted than ever, the cleansing of tears had flushed away his spiritual woe and he felt oddly renewed.

Now he had to do something.

He worried that day might break at any moment and would bring certain death. He was not as sure about the direction in which his head was pointing but was fairly certain that it aimed away from the enemy. He began to crawl, using his elbows and knees at first, gradually working up to his arms and legs. In little time he was swimming over the battlefield's great mounds of thrown-up earth and debris.

He could not stroke more than a few yards without bumping into a stiffening corpse and Ledyard gasped at each impromptu meeting with the dead. Some of the fallen were still alive. They elicited low moans or sighs when he collided with them, and it was at once heart-rending and horrifying to hear life leaking from those who were sure to die. He could do nothing to help them.

As he crawled around the dead and the dying Ledyard could feel panic building inside him again. The emotions that bedeviled his spirit were returning.

He got to his feet and started to walk, all the while fearing he would fall. The rising panic kept inducing him to run, but he could not commit himself. Instead Ledyard walked with long, hesitant strides as though crossing an expanse of thin ice. His nerve endings jangled with each step, and he began to tremble in apprehension of falling.

He did fall, flat on a dead man, and was just scrambling away when there was a boom in the distance, followed by the eerie whistle of an approaching shell. It flew over his head and exploded in a fiery burst several hundred yards away.

Ledyard cried out, "no . . . please no . . ." but his

entreaties were drowned by a steady cadence of distant booming followed by incoming shells that shrieked like a horde of banshees racing through the sky.

Shells were going off everywhere, and everywhere Ledyard ran his path was blocked by giant eruptions. His mind was jerking at every blast, and as he ran blindly to and fro, the circuits in his brain severed and shut off.

He fell into a hole, somersaulting down its walls to a pool of fetid water at the bottom. He splashed out, clambered over a dead body and tried to slither back up the slick wall. Above him the night barrage was reaching its height. There was nothing but fire and destruction and death, and halfway up the side of the hole he stopped moving. He turned onto his back and calmly sat up. He covered his ears with his hands and sank into a trauma far beyond tears.

He entered a realm devoid of emotion, a realm of unflinching paralysis. He had not just fallen into a hole, he had fallen all the way to the wretchedly barren floor of his soul. He sat on the side of the crater with the dead for company, not paying them any mind because he had lost the ability to think.

Many men in similar situations never fully regained the power of thought, but Ledyard would. It might have been sheer youth. Or it might have been something about his upbringing, an unseen quirk of personality or a sliver of will that could not be snapped. Undoubtedly, the mystery of his recovery in the crater was joined with the mystery of life. Ledyard was merely one of the lucky. Eventually the severed circuits repaired themselves, and he returned to grisly reality.

ESCAPE

Another artillery barrage brought Ledyard awake not long after first light. A nearby, upturned ration tin brimming with rainwater quenched his thirst, and while drinking it he was greatly relieved to find he was thinking clearly again. His body was working properly too, but was shivering from lack of food.

As shell after shell screamed overhead the ground shook like an ongoing, rolling earthquake. Ledyard hopped around the crater, going through the belongings of the dead. In one of the packs he found two cans of meat and a half- dozen biscuits all of which he gulped down, barely taking time to chew.

His knotted, shrunken stomach rebelled at the quantity forced upon it, regurgitating half the sustenance moments after it had ingested. The remaining half, Ledyard managed to keep down. He lay back against the crater and tried to concentrate on digestion, his body flinching every two or three seconds at the impact of shells.

He was still unable to gauge time and could not tell how long the latest round of artillery had lasted. He only realized it was over when he discovered that his body was still cringing sporadically without the accompaniment of sound or shaking earth.

When he felt that he had gotten his mental and physical parts to work in reasonable unison, Ledyard crept on hands and knees to the lip of the crater for a look out. All the way to the top he dreamed of seeing a friendly face. Nothing seemed sweeter than sharing a cigarette with a fellow soldier, and he was still hoping for some tiny miracle when he peered cautiously over the edge of the crater.

The enemy was advancing toward him. They were hurrying over the bombed out terrain like a great armada bounding over swells of the sea. The rain's moisture was evaporating in the sunshine adding shrouds of fog to the flat plains. The rushing fighters were appearing and disappearing like ghosts on the run.

He slid back down into the crater, assumed a grotesque posture and played dead. He could hear the suction of the mud as it swallowed their steps. He heard shouts uttered in guttural, alien language. Rifle fire increased as it passed him, reaching crescendo moments later that sounded as if all the firecrackers on earth were igniting at once.

The intense popping of small arms fire grew more and more distant. Still Ledyard waited, his lips pressed against the liquid earth, his heart pounding with trepidation. It was a long time before he raised his head and skittered back to the lip of the hole. The battlefield was devoid of movement, and for the first time since the preceding night he stood erect.

Then Ledyard stepped off into the clinging morass of mud that stretched as far as he could see.

In ten minutes, despite using the dead as stepping-stones, he had made only a few yards and with the passing of each minute's struggle his nerves worsened. At this pace he knew he would never escape the battlefield without being detected.

And he was afraid of the ooze beneath his feet. Twice Ledyard sank to his waist and it was only with the greatest exertion that he managed to extricate himself. Each time panic seized him. He might sink over his head and suffocate. An artillery shell might bury him as he tried to pull himself out. He might remain stuck until he lost his mind again. Or starved. Or died of thirst. An enemy might stop by and put a bullet in his brain while he stared helplessly down the muzzle of a rifle.

His progress was abruptly curtailed by another eruption of artillery fire, an uncounted number of big guns going off as one. Screaming shells tore through the air in a long, wailing cacophony.

Asking all that his body could give, Ledyard galloped through another ten feet of mire, rolled over the lip of a new crater and splashed into a deep pool of water. He pulled himself halfway out and clung to the sides of the hole as bombs exploded everywhere, producing great showers of mud that poured over him like syrup.

He held onto the slippery earth as a child clings to the bosom of its mother, and when the shelling finally ceased he continued to cling. The bombardment had plunged him back into the strange mode that knew only tension and fear. Again he had to steer himself back through the halting, delicate process of re-gathering his wits.

The small arms fire had never stopped, and when Ledyard finally opened his eyes and lifted his head he saw the half forms of desperate men stumbling past his hole. The enemy attack had failed. They were falling back.

Slowly, he reset his face against the mud and waited for absolute silence. When he was sure that all sound had vanished he pulled himself up and scanned the battlefield.

It was empty.

His hunger had returned and gazing back into the hole he saw that water filled three quarters of it. Several bodies were floating in the pool and Ledyard waded part way in to see what he could scavenge. The first body he tugged at was floating face down and turning it over he found himself staring into the face of his friend, Drayton Witt.

He felt nothing as he stared at the boy from Montana, neither surprise nor sadness. The words, "Aw Drayton . . . too bad" formed in his mind but they lacked any kind of color. The color had been washed out of Ledyard.

Dragging the corpse out of the water, he discovered that it was legless. He was unaffected. In the last twenty-four hours he had seen many people in pieces.

That Drayton was dead seemed normal. That he was missing his lower limbs seemed normal too.

As Ledyard went through Drayton's pockets looking for something to eat he found the tiny figure of a horse that his friend had whittled from a piece of wood. He decided to keep it, just for company, and slipped it into his shirt pocket.

By early afternoon he had completed a disappointing inventory of the floating dead, his efforts yielding but a single, soggy biscuit and a small tin of beef.

He was halfway through the tin when another round of shelling, this one more intense than any he had experienced before, drove him back to ground. He rode the shuddering, groaning earth for hours, and when the barrage ended he rolled onto his back and stared at the smoke-filled sky in disbelief that he could still be alive. Surely one of the thousands of shells that had gone off in his ears had found its way into his water-filled crater. At the very least he must now be buried alive.

But this could not be heaven and he could not think of anything he had done to deserve hell. Perhaps the true afterlife was a combination of the two or perhaps eternity was simply the place where a person died. That must be it, because Ledyard knew there was no way he could be alive.

Reinforcing this belief was a voice, a male voice repeating the same, single word in a foreign tongue. Reflexively, Ledyard looked toward the sound and glimpsed the joyous face of an angel peering down from the rim of the crater. Its grin never changing, the angel scooted down the wall of the hole and brought its face close to Ledyard's.

In the short span it took to perform this action, Ledyard realized that the angel was a German soldier. He wore no helmet and carried no gun and, though his uniform was caked in mud, an officer's insignia shone through at the collar.

"Hello brother," he said in German, maintaining a great, gap-toothed smile. He ran his hands quickly over Ledyard's body, causing him to recoil. Satisfied with the inspection the German clapped his hands together.

"Well . . . I see that you are just fine. You have no need of me." He spun his head around, spotted Drayton's corpse, slithered to its side, held its dead head between his hands and cried out happily, "Arise my brother!" Then he kissed the corpse full on the lips.

Ledyard watched in shocked silence as the lunatic

waded into the crater's pool and repeated his queer ministrations with the other bodies. When he had kissed them all, the soldier scrambled on all fours to the top of the crater. He stood for a few moments, his hands on his hips, scanning the battlefield eagerly. Then he stepped out of sight.

Curious, Ledyard scrambled after him. He lay on the crater's lip and watched the madman in action. Alternately rising and sinking in the mud, he made remarkable time as he struggled from body to body. At each of the dead he would throw up his hands in delight, as if he had encountered a long lost friend, sink to his knees, kiss the corpse, rise up and move on to the next.

Spellbound, Ledyard would have watched until he disappeared, but another barrage of artillery suddenly opened up. He could see the pattern of fire stitching closer and closer, but the lunatic was oblivious. A shell exploded near the self-appointed angel, sending a wave of mud fifty feet into the air and after it had settled back onto the earth the man was no longer visible. It was impossible to tell whether he had been killed by the impact or buried alive.

Ledyard shook his head lamentably and was beginning to ponder the insanity of war when the pop of rifle fire brought his head up. Surprising himself, he burst into laughter. The enemy was attacking again. Wave after wave was advancing toward him.

He slid back into the crater, submerged his waist in the water and hastily draped part of Drayton Witt's body over him. Then he settled down to wait. There was little panic in him now. He was worried to be sure but his heart did no pounding and his nerves didn't jangle. His biggest problem as the enemy neared was steeling himself against a surprisingly strong desire to giggle. The war had been reduced to a hideous game of hide and seek and he was fully in the spirit.

He was bolder now, and a few minutes after the sound of the advancing enemy had passed he rose and crawled to the top of the hole for a look.

For a long time he stared in the direction the enemy had gone. He could see or hear nothing and guessed correctly that they had succeeded in moving up.

There was a muffled boom somewhere in the distance behind him and when Ledyard turned to look he saw more of the enemy advancing. But there were very few of them, spaced far apart, and they were moving slowly.

Ledyard jumped back into the crater, ripped off a set of binoculars that hung around Drayton Witt's neck and scampered back to the rim.

Sighting through the glasses he found to his chagrin that the men coming in his direction were a clean-up crew, charged with destroying anyone they might find alive in the bomb holes that dotted the battlefield.

Occasionally, one of them would slip into a large crater and emerge moments later holding some souvenir of war high in the air, shouting his find to anyone within hearing. The soldiers were moving along like casual strollers, lobbing grenades into some of the holes, passing others. They didn't bother to inspect the holes, either before or after they dumped the deadly bombs.

Withdrawing to his original position, Ledyard again covered himself with Drayton's body and waited, listening as the explosions came closer. At last he could make out the slogging sound of footsteps. He shut his eyes and hoped with all his heart that he would be bypassed.

Something plopped next to him in the mud and Ledyard opened his eyes to see that a grenade had landed a foot from his face.

There was nothing to do but react. Sloughing off Drayton's corpse he lunged for the grenade, gripped it in one hand and gave it a mighty fling, watching as it sailed clear of the crater.

A man screamed curtly, the grenade detonated and there was a momentary silence, followed by distant shouting. Now he could hear others coming. Pulling Drayton over him like a blanket, Ledyard held his breath as they gathered somewhere above him and chattered back and forth, most likely offering opinions about what had happened.

A voice broke directly overhead and Ledyard knew that someone was looking into the crater. "Please don't let them come down here," he thought, "please, let them think he blew himself up."

Apparently, that's what the soldiers decided. After a few seconds someone uttered a few definitive words and there was silence, followed by the distinctive sucking sound of men walking in deep muck. The sucking sound grew fainter and Ledyard celebrated his triumph with a smile.

When he felt it was safe Ledyard shed his deathly bedding and dragged himself out of the pit for another look.

The big guns were booming as they always did at the front, but the sound was far away. It was heavenly to hear it so far away and it was heavenly to see the battlefield so still. For the first time since he had gone over the top, Ledyard felt himself relax. He gulped in a few long draughts of smokeless air and turned slowly about, making a complete survey of the landscape. There was no movement and no sound.

He knew that he was now behind enemy lines, but whatever problems came he would have to race for life as they came. For now he needed water and food and a way out, a way that would lead him to some kind of shelter.

As the sun started to descend, Ledyard picked his way across no-man's land, shopping as he went. The bodies of the fallen yielded a good bounty: food, water, a rifle, a backpack full of hand grenades and an unopened package of cigarettes.

When twilight came he had been walking on nearly solid ground for almost an hour. The land was still flat but he noticed that flecks of green were poking through the earth.

Pausing to take a drink, he shaded his eyes and saw what looked like a copse of trees rising up on the horizon.

As he walked in that direction Ledyard did not think of being captured or shot or blown up. His feet were moving with a pleasing lightness over ever-firmer ground, and he made for what he now confirmed to be trees, trees with real, living leaves. He could think only of how grateful he was to be out of the horrible mud.

And of course he was abundantly happy to be alive. That went without saying, or even thinking. To feel his arms swinging, his eyes seeing, his lungs breathing, his heart beating, was enough. He didn't need to revel in how lucky he was. It wasn't Ledyard's style to be cocky anyway. He'd always felt being cocky was about the best way in the world to jinx yourself.

IN THE TREES

By the time he made the edge of the woods, walking consisted solely of forcing one foot to follow another. Every cell clamored for rest, but finding the edge of the woods partially destroyed he willed himself deeper into the trees. The ground rose slightly upward as he staggered toward its apex. The trees were so thick that they were only inches apart in places, but on reaching the top they opened into a tiny clearing. There Ledyard collapsed, falling into a deep sleep almost as he hit the ground.

When he woke his nose was filled with the wholesome fragrance of young grass. Something was climbing his earlobe and reaching back he captured a small, green beetle that he studied as it navigated the creases in his palm. He watched the beetle with a wonder he had not known since childhood. What a marvel it was in all its aspects. And what a delight to watch something whole, a creature at peace with itself and its environment.

A bird sang, and shading his eyes against the bright sunlight, he quickly found it standing on a low limb a few feet above him. The bird too filled him with a sense of awe. It fluffed its feathers, breathed through its mouth, swiveled its head, hopped from foot to foot and cocked a round, wet eye at Ledyard, singing all the time. He got the feeling that the bird was performing for him, showing all the magnificent things it could do, and when it leapt into space and took flight Ledyard made light applause with his hands.

He stared up through the trees and reckoned the angle of the sun put the life of day past noon. He opened a tin of beef, washed it down with half a canteen of water, brushed the dried mud from his uniform, removed all traces of it's presence, and set off to explore the woods.

The reconnaissance did not take long. The trees were not so much a woods as they were an island, roughly rectangular in shape. Though he was not good at figuring such things, Ledyard estimated that he was hidden in two or three acres of trees.

On each side there was open space. One led back into no-man's land. The other faced an open meadow, maybe half a mile across, which fed into the flight line of a small, enemy air base.

Beyond the wide meadow was another line of trees, but there was no way to tell how deep they might be. He would have to cross to them at nightfall, and Ledyard sat at the edge of the trees smoking cigarettes as he watched what little activity there was at the sleepy airfield. During the time he watched, which was much of the afternoon, only one plane swooped down the length of the long meadow and landed.

It was late afternoon before he started back, his plan being to sleep awhile before crossing the meadow in the middle of night. As he walked up the incline it occurred to him that it would be a nice idea to sit out the war in this little wood. His mind jumped a step further, entertaining the thought that it wouldn't be bad to spend the rest of his life here. He hadn't been in the war very long, but it had been enough to sour him on the whole human race. Individuals were one thing, people like Drayton Witt, but the race itself, when left to its own devices . . . a tremor of loathing ran up his spine.

Humankind was a wash. This never-ending war had been deadlocked for years, long before the Americans jumped into it. There were no winners when it came to a conflict like the Great War. The biggest dolt to ever wear a uniform could see that. The best an individual could hope for was to somehow survive it. The best the world could hope for was that it would somehow burn itself out someday. Humankind had distinguished itself in but two ways, Ledyard thought. It had demonstrated a tremendous capacity for incompetence and an insatiable appetite for carnage.

"Ledyard, the beetles and the birds," he thought, chuckling to himself. "That beats anything going on outside these trees."

His idyll was broken by the sounds of bright, happy voices, German voices, filtering down to him from the high point in the wood. Freezing, Ledyard listened, trying to get a fix on them. After a few seconds, he could tell that the voices were stationary.

He glanced about him. There was silence from everywhere but above. He crept forward on all fours, taking great care to make no sound with his hands or knees. A few minutes of crawling brought him close enough to see the heads of men, pilots from the airfield he guessed. They were the picture of confident, Germanic youth, and they were picnicking in the very spot he had made his bed the night before.

He contemplated tossing one of his grenades into their midst but the more he thought about it the less it appealed to him. What could he possibly gain from doing something like that? Practically, it would be nothing but a blazing, noisy advertisement for himself, only hastening his own death. And what would blowing up a group of picnicking pilots actually accomplish? Would it shorten the war? He thought not.

A strange thought popped into his head. Who won didn't matter nearly so much as putting an end to wholesale destruction. That would be the greatest victory of all. And the only one.

Keeping his eyes on the pilots, Ledyard backtracked down the slope. When he was out of their view he got to his feet and tramped to the far end of the wood, looking for a spot where he could conceal himself. He found a deadfall not far from the meadow and after thirty minutes of digging out a hollow he had constructed a safe, dry chamber. He wedged himself in, covering the opening as thoroughly as possible. Folding his arms in front of his chest, he shut his eyes and began to rehearse the nocturnal trek he would make when the moon was up and the war was asleep.

His own sleep was so deep and so luxurious that he barely stirred. When he finally opened his eyes again it was daylight. Ledyard groaned with dismay as he pushed away the branches that covered his hiding place.

He sat on the log that had sheltered him and fished out the remaining pieces of gray meat floating in his last tin of beef. Then he drank the grease and swallowed what was left of his water.

"Well, now I'm in for it," he thought, pushing an errant drop of water from his lip back into his mouth.

It was early morning, and he would have to go thirsty and hungry all day before making his getaway. In the meantime he would check the clearing at the top of the hill for scraps left behind by the picnickers.

Lifting himself off the log, he thought of the meadow again and gazed in that direction with the idea of re-estimating its width and the time it would take to get across.

A riderless horse was standing just beyond the tree line, its neck arching over the earth as it nibbled the most promising shoots of grass. It wore no saddle but a bridle was intact about its head, the reins trailing lazily behind as the horse browsed.

Ledyard moved to the edge of the trees and the horse jerked its head up and stared at him.

"Hello there," Ledyard said softly, raising his hand in a gesture of peace.

The horse stared a moment longer then returned to its browsing. Ledyard took a step forward and the animal moved a step in the opposite direction.

"Typical," Ledyard thought. If there was one thing he knew about horses it was that they loved playing hard to get. Many animals used that behavior as an everyday form of revenge on the human race, but horses were the masters.

He watched the animal a few moments longer, gauging the sincerity of his aloofness. The horse was watching him too and Ledyard decided that his commitment was flimsy.

"Okay," he called softly, "I'll see you then."

He walked the few steps back to the deadfall. On the

way he glanced over his shoulder. The horse's head was up, watching him go.

Ledyard rolled under the log and waited. It wasn't long before he heard the first tentative footfalls of the big animal as it moved into the trees. Not wanting to startle him, Ledyard began to hum a little tune. The plop of his footsteps came closer and closer, then stopped. Ledyard twisted slowly out from his hiding place and looked up, straight into the curious face hanging over him. The horse was peering down from the other side of the log.

"Hi," Ledyard said, getting to his feet.

He stretched out a hand and let the horse sniff his fingers. Then he sat down submissively on the log and began to stroke his soft muzzle, gently taking up one of the free hanging reins in the process.

The horse was perfectly amenable to being captured and stood still as Ledyard made a tour of his body, running hands over the neck, withers, back, rump, legs and belly. The horse carried no wounds and had good muscle. He'd been shod recently and his short, dark coat glistened with good health. Whoever had been in charge of him had kept him in excellent shape.

"You one of ours or one of theirs?" Ledyard asked when he reached his head again.

The horse looked at him quizzically. "Too smart to answer, eh?" The horse sighed deeply and gazed off through the trees as if he couldn't be bothered with such trivialities. Laughing at his new companion's disdain, Ledyard laid a hand on his neck and said, "Well, let's take a walk."

He stepped forward and the horse, with an ease that might have indicated years of togetherness, stepped right along with him.

They revisited the scene of the pilot's picnic but found nothing but a flock of yellow-eyed blackbirds. The grass was good, and Ledyard let the horse browse until he lost interest. Then they made a round of inspections.

The no-man's land from which Ledyard had emerged was still a graveyard and the airfield was sleepy as ever.

Ledyard wanted to distance himself from the enemy and they tramped the length of the trees, stopping at the end furthest from the airfield, there to wait for night.

By mid-afternoon the horse was becoming impatient with waiting and Ledyard, knowing he was getting thirsty, tried to keep him moving.

His own thirst had become profound. He had even put a pebble under his tongue to stimulate saliva and keep his mouth moist, but hours had passed and a little wetness on his tongue was no longer enough. He was having trouble thinking about anything but water.

The tension was building in both of them and, though it was still two hours before sunset, Ledyard decided he would get onto the horse's back. At the least it would break the monotony of waiting. And it would tell him something about who was going to carry him across half a mile of meadow after dark.

Taking the reins in one hand, he patted the horse's back to let him know what was coming and swung up. The transformation in his compliant companion was instantaneous and remarkable.

The horse tucked his chin toward his chest and began to dance slowly in place, every muscle at the ready. He was coiling for action, but at the same time was not at all unmanageable. Ledyard cued him with light pressure from one heel and they moved off through the trees. His walk was more like a glide, free and airy yet beautifully controlled. His mouth was extraordinarily light, the slightest tug on the reins inducing him to halt. After a few steps Ledyard knew that he was sitting astride an animal that was superior in every way.

The clank and grind of heavy equipment was droning in the distance. They halted and listened. A few more steps brought them within view of the battlefield, a view that revealed a terrible spectacle.

Dozens of tanks, escorted by hundreds of ground troops were headed their way. To one man on a horse it looked like half the German army was coming.

Wheeling about, they hurried back the way they had come. When they reached the apron of the meadow again Ledyard tried to think of suitable options but nothing was available. There would be no way to conceal himself from what was coming and what was coming would be here long before dark.

With a cluck to the horse they moved onto the meadow at a calculated walk. If they were seen by anyone at the airfield a walk was more likely to arouse curiosity than suspicion.

They had traveled barely fifty yards when Ledyard heard an engine start up and seconds later a bi-plane was lifting shakily into the air. Ledyard cursed his luck. Not only had someone decided to put a plane up at the same time he was crossing but the wind had conspired against him as well. It was coming his way.

The fragile plane, bobbing like a cork in the air, would pass directly overhead in a few seconds. Ledyard glanced at the trees in the distance. There was no way he could make it without being seen, and it was too late to go back. He walked on, watching the approach of the plane from the corner of his eye.

Its nose dropped and it swerved toward him to get a look at the man on the horse.

Ledyard could no longer ignore the oncoming plane. Pulling up he stood and waited as the aircraft sunk lower and lower, its blurred propeller aimed directly at him.

He had planned to wave but as the plane zoomed in he sensed a lethal intent. His arm had just gone into the air when he made a last second decision to bolt. Spinning around, they shot toward the trees from whence they had come, Ledyard laying low on the horse's neck.

His sixth sense saved both their lives. Just as they dug for the trees the plane's machine gun opened up, spraying deadly fire over the spot they had occupied.

The horse's speed was tremendous and they regained the trees in what seemed like no time. Holding him with one hand Ledyard placed the other on his rump and twisted his head for a look back. The plane had already climbed high into the sky and was executing a long, lazy turn. It was coming back.

As he watched it drop back down to skim the surface of the meadow Ledyard felt certain that it was not going to bother hunting for him in the trees. It was going to land and report the sighting.

Reaching over his shoulder, he pulled one of the grenades out of the pack on his back. Grabbing up a hunk of the horse's mane he waited until what he thought was the opportune moment and digging his heels into the horse's flanks, burst back into the open at a full run. His hope was to try to intersect the plane at a right angle, thereby avoiding the machine gun.

The plane lurched awkwardly in his direction but was too late to meet him dead on. As they came together he could see the goggled faces of two men staring at him from the cockpit.

Ledyard sat straight up on the running horse, pulled the pin with his teeth and heaved the bomb as high and far into the air as he could.

The grenade exploded in mid-air, near one of the wing tips. It did not hit the plane and for a moment Ledyard thought he had failed. But either the concussion or the surprise of his attack caused one of the wings to dip crazily toward the earth. As the aircraft's wing dropped lower and lower, Ledyard pulled up to watch.

By the time it reached the vicinity of the air field it was flying practically perpendicular to the ground and Ledyard knew it was going to crash. Suddenly, it cartwheeled onto its nose, bounced into the air and came to ground with a faint, reverberating thud.

Ledyard and the horse galloped for the tree line and when they made the woods he pulled up and looked down the meadow for the last time. There were flames and a column of black smoke, billowing into the sky above the airfield.

THE WANDERERS

When they had disappeared into the cover of the woods Ledyard jumped down to check his mount. The animal had exhausted himself with the race across the meadow and was dripping with sweat. Ledyard pinched the skin on his neck and watched as it slowly flattened out to its original position, a telltale sign of dehydration.

Ledyard walked, and the horse followed him through the trees. The going was made easy by the deep cushion of leaves under their feet and the extreme height of the old growth towering over their heads. Shafts of sunlight penetrated here and there but the air was cooler by ten or fifteen degrees.

They had been traveling for half an hour when they happened on a sunlit, overgrown clearing. Its surface was oddly depressed, as if an errant bomb had landed there some years before. Several inches of rainwater, coated with floating leaves, had not yet evaporated and they settled down to drink, Ledyard on one side, the horse on the other.

Though he wanted to empty the pool and then suck the mud, Ledyard did not want to vomit and forced himself to stop after a few mouthfuls.

Rolling onto his side, he lay on a bed of green at the edge of the water and watched the horse drink, enraptured by his placid beauty. The animal was balanced neatly on all four feet, his eyes half-closed in ecstasy. His square, sensitive lips seemed to barely touch the surface. Motionlessly, they sucked huge swallows which Ledyard could see as they traveled the length of his neck like stones tumbling rhythmically down a sluice.

For awhile the horse did not look up, and when he did his gaze traveled straight to the man on the other side of the water with an expression so supremely content that Ledyard could not help smiling. Then he lowered his head, nibbled briefly at the water and drank some more.

A sudden wave of longing swept over the young soldier. He felt an overwhelming desire to climb on the horse's back and ride out of the war. They would ride together for however long it took, without water or food or sleep, ride until they reached a place something like the spot they now occupied.

There they would see to nothing but their mutual care. And when they grew weary of living, they would lie down back to back on a bed of grass and breath their last together. How fine it would be for man and animal to achieve such equality.

He sat up on crossed legs, looked at the horse and felt his heart swell. "I love you," he thought. "I never loved anything so much in my life. I am so happy."

With a parting glance the horse turned away from the water and began to clip the green morsels of grass at his feet.

"I'm going to call you Drayton," Ledyard said to himself. Then, in the same way a moron might mouth a sentence, he whispered faintly, "Drayton . . . that's good."

The horse meandered toward the center of the clearing and, as he did, sunlight splashed over his rump revealing an out of place pink line several inches long coursing over the top of his round hips.

Jumping to his feet, Ledyard joined him in the clearing and on closer inspection found that Drayton had been hit.

The slug had plowed a superficial furrow across the top of Drayton's hindquarters, shearing off a neat line of hair and splitting the uppermost layer of skin. What little bleeding there was had already stopped and caked.

Ledyard took off his shirt, dipped a sleeve in the rainwater and washed the crease thoroughly. He didn't want insects to feed on the cut, and to stymie them he scooped a small handful of mud from the floor of the pool and dabbed it meticulously along the pink line.

None of these attentions were wholly necessary. The wound was trifling and Drayton would have healed perfectly had nothing been done. But it mattered greatly to Ledyard. The aid he provided for Drayton was aid for himself, a first building block in the restoration of his own humanity and faith.

The foundations of war, dominance and conquest, had never been part of his drive. Ledyard had always been attracted to the subtler, long-term values of a sentient way of life. Now, in the form of an animal, he had the opportunity to indulge sweetness, even in the midst of war, and he was reaching for beauty as surely as a pilgrim reaches for salvation.

Of course Ledyard did not articulate these ideas, even in thought. He was merely a young man whose desire to love and be loved had been triggered by a chance encounter with a fellow creature in an environment of horror. But now that the mechanism had been tripped he wanted to love with a fullness previously unknown to him.

Ledyard slipped off Drayton's bridle and lay down on the bare ground, using his grenade pack as a pillow. Hunger had made him light-headed, and as he waited for sleep to come he wished again that if he and Drayton were going to die that they would do so together.

What if they lived? When he heard Drayton go to ground with a grunt Ledyard made a solemn vow. If they lived they would do so together. No war, no sickness, no circumstances, no matter how inconceivable, would separate them.

To stay with Drayton was the clearest goal he had ever imagined, a purpose that he could see himself fighting for or dying for without question or qualm. As he slipped toward sleep that night, wrapped in his own arms, he could not remember having felt so clear and so good about his place in the world.

The feeling was gone when he opened his eyes at dawn. The dull distant thud of artillery was beating out the same cadence it always did, a sound as omnipotent at the front as surf on the shore. Listening to reverberating rhythm irritated Ledyard. It made him feel he had been dreaming about his place in the world. But something far worse had happened.

Drayton was gone.

Ledyard called his name but heard no answering nicker and for a moment he felt crushed with hopelessness.

Sitting up, he eyed the empty woods, cursing himself inwardly for entertaining such foolish and exalted notions of fanciful love between man and animal. What could he have been thinking? He must have been unhinged.

A movement in the trees suddenly struck his eyes. Drayton was there after all, and when he saw Ledyard sitting up, the horse walked straight back, lowered his head to within a few inches of Ledyard's and snorted as if to say, "I've been waiting for you." Ledyard smiled and stroked the corner of Drayton's mouth, but practical concerns suddenly overpowered his joy.

He was lost. And he was behind enemy lines. It was real. He couldn't dream the war away. If he stayed where he was, someone would eventually find him sitting in the woods and kill him.

But when he looked up he could only see Drayton's soft, wet eyes. The affection and respect he felt came rushing back. There was something about being in the presence of this animal that made him feel absolutely pure in his heart. He would not . . . he could not . . . lose such a feeling.

His dilemma remained however. The war and Drayton were intrinsically opposing forces and Ledyard could not imagine how he could honor Drayton and accede to the war.

Pulling the bridle over Drayton's ears, he concluded that there was no way that he, one puny human, could hope to resolve such weighty issues in a wood somewhere in Belgium, surrounded by the greatest human conflict the world had ever known.

He felt weak as he swung onto Drayton's back and knew it was vital to focus on what really demanded his attention . . . the need to get food into his stomach.

They pushed off through the woods, continuing in a direction that led away from the airfield. Despite his hunger, Ledyard decided they would stay in the trees for an hour or more before exploring what lay beyond them, thinking it would be better to starve a little longer than risk detection.

The traveling was so good that Ledyard forgot about the war. The constant thump of artillery was relegated to background noise, and soon he was conscious only of Drayton's footfalls on the forest floor and the vocalizing of birds. The sky, when he could glimpse it, was cloudless and strikingly blue and for a time the illusion that they might be the only horse and man on earth brought a tranquility to mind that allowed him to meditate solely on the beauty surrounding him.

Intermittently, he worked on getting to know as much as he could about Drayton. He spoke to him in low, kindly tones and Drayton listened, flicking his ears back and forth as the words reached them.

Instead of using the reins, Ledyard tried changing directions with a shifting of weight or pressure from a knee as they meandered through the trees. He was amazed at the machine-like precision with which Drayton responded even to the subtlest cues.

A whispered "whoa" resulted in an instantaneous halt and a single cluck from between Ledyard's teeth prompted an unhesitating step forward. He tried jumping off while they were moving and found that Drayton stopped as soon as his own feet hit the ground. Then he would wait, still as a statue, until Ledyard swung onto his back. If the wait seemed inordinately long he would turn his head and gaze at his companion with an expression that said, "Well . . ."

Ledyard tried stretching out full, using Drayton's beautiful, high backside as a headrest. The horse continued his amble through the forest without missing a beat.

Ledyard backed him and spun him. He held him and he let him go. He hung on his neck and slid off his hindquarters. He lay across his spine, held his feet in his hands and crawled back and forth under his belly. Drayton didn't fuss, nor did he resist. He never took advantage and he never panicked. He was perfect.

Through his entire upbringing Ledyard had been taught to respect animal life, and he felt that Drayton was responding in part to this respect. He knew too that Drayton had been well trained, but there was something about this horse that superseded training or the kindness of a stranger. It was a quality manifested in every movement of his trim, supple frame. It was present in his well-tuned mind, his fathomless eyes, his economy of movement and his steady breath.

The quality was confidence, and Ledyard was convinced that it was a confidence too supreme to have been bestowed by the hand of man. Drayton had to have been born with it.

"Drayton . . . what you have cannot be given and it can not be taken away." He extended a hand and stroked the animal's neck. "What you are, Drayton, is a wonder. . . . You are a wonder horse." When the sun was at its height, they changed course, making a hard right

that Ledyard calculated would take them out of the center of the forest. He had hoped that he could find some scraps in the heart of the woods, but had discovered nothing but a rusting, German helmet.

In a few minute's time the trees began to thin out, and shortly after that the two wanderers reached the border of a great desolate plain, broken by mounds of twisted rubble and the occasional erect splinter of what had once been a tree. The destruction was so complete that Ledyard surmised the ground before him had been contested for years.

The battlefield was silent as a graveyard and Ledyard felt briefly like a tourist, contemplating some man-made phenomenon. His mind reeled at the thought of how much ordnance it had taken to create such monumental waste.

"Millions upon millions," he thought. It must be that many for he knew that millions of French and Germans and Russians had already been killed.

There was an object several hundred yards in front of him and, lifting the binoculars, Ledyard recognized it as a tank. The machine's nose was positioned at a slight, upward angle and there was a huge cut along its top, as if it had been cleaved by a gigantic ax.

He walked Drayton back a little deeper into the trees where the grass was better and pulled the bridle off. When the horse was well into his browsing Ledyard gave him a reassuring pat and walked onto the sun-splashed battleground.

The heat of the day, combined with his own famished state, made the going hard and Ledyard had sweated through his uniform by the time he reached the rusting hulk that had once been a factory-smooth war machine. Standing at the rear of the tank he peered through the rupture.

Several crewmen were still inside. Two of the bodies wore French helmets on their smooth skulls. Part of a ribcage poked through the rotting seams of one uniform, the vertebrae of a backbone through another. A fiendish hand clutched a lever and from the mouth of the same man hung a set of dentures. The tank's innards were beyond the ken of human experience, as if it were the methodical satire of ghouls.

Portions of the interior were blackened, but the flames had not engulfed the entire vehicle and in the dark recesses of its walls Ledyard could make out storage containers. Taking care not to cut himself on the shards of jagged metal that guarded the entrance, Ledyard climbed inside.

He lifted the bodies up as he reached them, tossing the carcasses over the side. One by one they struck the ground with a bony clatter, like sacks of kindling.

As he went about the foul work, Ledyard wondered what the remnants might have represented. A brilliant student? A talented sculptor? A friendly butcher who would raise a family of seven? An African adventurer who would someday have commanded the world's attention? A national leader? A future inventor of some marvelous contraption that would revolutionize the way people lived? An anonymous soul who would work the same job for thirty years and pursue crossword solutions in retirement? Whether grand or small the potential was now wasted forever, reduced to nothing more than trashy trifles littering the earth.

And what of Ledyard Dixon? Ledyard Dixon had not meditated much on his own future. There was nothing in particular he had wanted to do with his life. Until now it had been enough to be young and vital.

He liked the way Uncle Cecil lived, happily creating something out of nothing with brushes and paint. But aside from making a few drawings as every child does, Ledyard had neither discernible talent nor any direction in which to take it.

He leaned out over the tank and studied the human remains he had scattered on the ground. It was not too much to think that one of them had been a young fellow no different that himself . . . the only difference being that one was now bones while the other still possessed flesh and blood. A tremor of dread flickered up his spine.

"Maybe that will be me . . . killed and never found, never mourned, never celebrated. Why is it not me? Why am I standing here looking down? Why am I still alive? Does it matter that I am?"

When he had cleared the last of the bodies, Ledyard wiped the perspiration from his face with a shirtsleeve and lifted the binoculars for a look back at the woods. Drayton was still there, munching grass.

Sinking to a squat, he made a careful inspection of the tank. Along one wall, still lashed to the sides with metal bindings, were what looked like petrol canisters. He was right about the first three but when he unscrewed the cap of the fourth he did not smell fuel. He dipped a finger into the liquid and tasted it with the tip of his tongue. It was water. Five gallons of water.

On the opposite wall he found fifty feet of good rope, a well-stocked medical kit and a dented metal box half the size of a small valise. Inside, stacked in two neat rows, one atop the other, were a variety of tins, all of them containing items of food. There was beef and chicken and vegetables and potatoes, sardines and cake and, in one can, wafers of dark chocolate.

He devoured the contents of two ration cans, chewing and swallowing slowly. He drank some of the tepid water and watched Drayton through the glasses while he smoked a cigarette.

His strength returned rapidly and in ten minutes Ledyard was back on the ground, fashioning a sled from a flat piece of metal. On this he secured the big water can and the box of rations. He made a harness out of the rope he had found, placed one of the French helmets on his head, and dragged his goods back across the battlefield and into the woods.

Using the helmet as a vessel, he let Drayton drink half the water. The rest he poured into four canteens he had salvaged from the tank.

He had also brought back a pencil and a blank page of a handbook he had found in the wreck. When Drayton began to graze again Ledyard stretched out on a bed of leaves and went to work on a map.

Starting with the forward observation trench he sketched the enemy lines, the no-man's land from which he had made his miraculous escape, the island of trees, the airfield, the long meadow, the woods he and Drayton had traveled through and the tank that marked his present position. He did his best to estimate the distance between all these points and his rough computations indicated that he was now five or six miles from his original starting point.

Directions were more difficult to ascertain but, rummaging through memories of where the sun had been at various times, he was able to make a guess at what course he would have to take if he were to have the barest chance of reaching the American lines. Of course he could not count on the allied position being in the same place. The German attack must have pushed them back but, given the slow ebb and flow of trench warfare, he reckoned they had not receded much, probably no more than a mile.

Through most of the afternoon Ledyard calculated and recalculated, a process made agonizing with the knowledge that he really had no sure idea of where he might be.

Finally, he decided on a course of action. It was based solely on his estimate of the direction in which he would find the Americans and he figured they lay somewhere to the south. He would continue north until he intersected a road, taking it east until he found a likely thruway, fields or another stand of woods. Then he would turn about and head south.

Exhausted by so many dubious equations, Ledyard rolled onto his back, covered his face with the French helmet, and fell asleep thinking how lucky he was that the moon was coming full. At least they would be able to see where they were going.

The light in the forest was flecked with gold when he woke. Drayton lay a few yards away, stretched out full along the ground, snoring blissfully. Ledyard cleared his throat and the horse sat up, throwing his forelegs in front of him. When Ledyard rose, Drayton did the same. He shook the twigs and leaves off his back, ambled over to where Ledyard was standing and nudged at the water can with his nose.

As they drank and ate, the lengthening, melancholy shadows of the forest matched Ledyard's darker turn of heart. He knew that these moments would be the last they would share in the security of the trees. Making it back to the safety of friendly forces would necessitate a naked, almost helpless exposure to the vicious world of war and Ledyard wished mightily that some way could be found to just stay put. But it was hopeless.

There was nothing to sustain them here, and the idea of cringing in a grove of trees went against his grain. Hiding and seeking was all right given no other alternative, but hiding as an action unto itself was unacceptable.

Ledyard had been a dreamer, sometimes to a fault he supposed, but even being a dreamer was worlds away from measuring out life in fear of sound or sight.

He thought again of surrender, going so far as to visualize how easy it would be. A white flag, an approach from afar and a simple raising of his hands was all it would take. He might yet be shot, but if made the right overtures in broad daylight with many of the enemy looking on, he doubted that giving himself up would be more traumatic than having his hands tied behind his back. Of course he would be hauled off to a camp, some scene of starvation and despair, but he knew he could endure lice and gruel and even cruelty. Any deprivation seemed easy compared to facing a thousand infantry with a sack of grenades.

The morality of surrender caused him no anguish either. He had not been long at the front, but he had already seen all that he needed to see. The war was a game, having nothing to do with duty or honor or the suppression of evil. He had not only seen the face of war, he had felt its skin and tasted its blood and slept in its bed. He had held hands with war and found that there was not one iota of glory in it. War was nothing but an exercise . . . a competition to determine which side could waste more resources.

It was a grinding wheel, turning all it touched to grist, and the wheel kept on revolving because the captains of industry saw profit there. The longer the wheel turned the longer the profits piled up. Each dead man was replaced with a new man wearing a new uniform, toting a new rifle, marching in new boots, drinking from a new canteen. And on and on right down to the stamps on the letters.

He could find no cowardice in surrendering. To Ledyard's mind there was probably more honor in surrender than there was in continuing to fight. Continuing to fight served only one purpose. It kept the war alive and would do so until each side was too exhausted to go on. Then there would be peace.

"What will the face of peace look like?" Ledyard asked himself already knowing the answer. "Peace will look like that out there."

He turned to look at the battlefield beyond the trees. "It will look like skeletons in uniform, men without legs, rusting tanks, dead trees, dead earth. Peace will be a desert." The conclusion was inescapable. Surrender was not only honorable, it was patently logical under Ledyard's circumstances. Nothing could be gained by sacrificing himself.

But it was impossible.

The reason was standing a foot away. Briefly, Ledyard wished he and Drayton had never found each other. He wished his feelings did not run so deep. It would be so much easier to be callously pragmatic. He should say to himself, "After all, it's just a horse," and be done with it but to think that would deny what he truly felt. Drayton was beauty and intelligence and innocence and friendship. He was the embodiment of what Ledyard regarded as love in all its splendor. How could he disavow what was sacred above all else?

Drayton too was viewing the landscape outside the trees, his ears pricked, his eyes working at the peak of their powers. As Ledyard watched the object of his affection a new line of thought began to form in his mind, a line of thought as deflating as it was profound.

Through all his grand ruminations, through all the heart-felt swelling in his breast, he had not really been considering Drayton. Ledyard realized in a bright flare of consciousness that he had only been considering himself. If he loved this animal so much then why was he on the verge of putting him in mortal danger? Did it really matter whose hands he might fall into so long as he lived? Wasn't keeping Drayton alive in the world what mattered most?

While the sun set Ledyard quickly gathered the items he needed. Drayton stood still, watching him pensively. The young soldier glanced about in a last check of his surroundings. Then, shouldering the rifle, he approached the horse and looked him in the eye. "I'm leaving Drayton . . . and you're staying." Drayton did not move a muscle. He only blinked as Ledyard spoke. "I'm going now," Ledyard whispered, a lump crowding his throat. "I love you."

When he turned away Drayton came after him, and Ledyard hesitated.

"Stay Drayton," he said firmly. Again Drayton moved when Ledyard did. The boy gently pushed the horse's face to one side and put the full weight of his body against the point where neck met shoulder. "C'mon Drayton," he grunted, "don't make this harder than it already is." Once he was turned, Ledyard placed both hands on Drayton's rump and shoved him forward. The horse took a half-hearted step, twisted his head and looked back at Ledyard.

Exasperated, Ledyard threw up his hands, whooping and hollering and lunging forward with as much menace as he could show.

Startled, Drayton trotted a few yards into the trees, his

tail raised, his neck bowed, his nostrils in full blow. Then he turned and, seeing that nothing was actually wrong, started back.

Ledyard screamed, "Drayton stay!" The horse stopped. "Stay, stay, stay," Ledyard shouted. Then he turned and strolled quickly out of the woods. On reaching the battlefield, he turned north at a run and covered another fifty yards before looking back.

Drayton was just coming out of the trees. He too turned north and came ahead at a fast walk, his head swinging back and forth as he glanced nervously at the battlefield, then at the woods. He looked lost and scared.

Ledyard's heart bled for the bewildered animal, and a moment later he was walking back to meet him.

"I'm sorry Drayton," he said, cradling the long face in both hands. "I was just thinking of you . . . I guess you were thinking of me."

With that he gently turned Drayton around and they walked back to find his bridle.

The moon came up almost as night fell, a great yellow disc rising off the horizon. Artillery flashed in the distance, but this sector of the war zone was otherwise very still and they rode under the big moon in perfect peace.

After half an hour the battlefield's topography began to change. More and more bare trees began to appear, their skeletons throwing macabre silver shadows across the wasted ground. The forest thrived a few feet to his left, while it lay in ruin a few feet to his right. It was as though they were traveling a literal line between life and death.

When they stopped to rest Ledyard, found the queer landscape irresistible. Holding the French helmet under Drayton's mouth, his eyes roamed the eerie panorama that sprawled before him.

Something seemed out of place with one of the trees. It was at least a hundred yards off, but even at distance he could see that an unusual number of its graceful limbs had been spared of the shelling and there seemed to be something hanging in them. Ledyard lifted his binoculars but their lenses showed less than what he could see with the naked eye.

He started to mount, but as he placed a hand on Drayton's withers he could not resist looking again. Something was definitely hanging there in the moonlight. A plane perhaps. Possibly a balloon. It was too big to be a body.

The battleground was spookier once he was in it. The grotesque terrain was a patchwork of brilliant light intermingled with inky pools of gloom.

Though he saw no dead, the ground was peppered with thousands of pieces of jagged metal and he was glad he had left Drayton behind. This was no place for the delicate feet of a horse.

It was no place for a man either, and as Ledyard moved closer to the object of his curiosity he felt more and more cut off. The tangled shape of the shattered trees seemed to possess a queer life of their own and when the dry tendril of a limb inadvertently grabbed at his shirtsleeve, he jumped away with a shriek.

The big tree was in front of him now but he still could not determine what bulky object hung in its branches. Most of it was sunk in shadow. He stepped around the tree as he reached it and gazed up into the eyeless face of a horse sparkling in the moonlight.

The head and neck of the animal was facing up and its

physical attitude gave the impression of flight, as though it had been trying to climb higher as it died.

But as Ledyard stared at the ghastly image he realized it had done no climbing. The force of some massive explosion had blown it into the tree.

Its mouth was open, frozen in a scream of horror. The viscera and muscle and organs were gone. What remained was a husk. The sun-dried skin, still blotched with hair, was stretched taut over its skeleton, the bones of which had begun to peek through. Most of the faded, black mane and all of its tail remained. Two shriveled hind legs dangled in space. The front ones were gone.

Seeing its forelock made Ledyard immensely sad. The jaunty little forelock was still falling down the horse's face, its wisps fluttering in the evening breeze between orbs that had once held deep, gentle eyes.

The specter of a horse perched in a tree was a preposterous sight. But that was not the reason Ledyard stood his ground as the minutes rolled by.

Unlike his human counterparts, he had not come into the war on his own volition. The horse in the tree had been forced into the terror of battle, used and discarded without an inkling of what was happening to him. And he had not only been reduced to death. He had been left to decompose in a tree like some lurid, carnival attraction for all the world to see and to mock.

Gritting his teeth, Ledyard started into the tree, climbing hand over hand until he was face to face with the dead horse. He reached out and brushed the dusty skin on its dry nose with his fingertips. An idea came to him and he dipped into a shirt pocket for Drayton Witt's wooden carving and tied the tiny figure in the forelock of the dead animal. Then he patted the horse's forehead and climbed down.

As he made his way back to Drayton, Ledyard's stride was brisk and purposeful. He did not know precisely what had driven him to climb the tree and do what he did. He had done it because he knew no one else would, and that was reason enough.

When he saw Drayton, standing patiently where he had left him in the moonlight, Ledyard's determination had galvanized into something new and hard.

He would protect this horse with every ember of his spirit, protect him from the senseless agonies that seemed to inundate the whole world.

It came to Ledyard that night that his one ambition in life was to devote himself to beauty, and as they moved deeper into the north he vowed that any fighting he did from this moment forward would be in the service of beauty and nothing else.

RUNNING

The moon had begun to wane when the line of trees that had flanked them for so long finally ran out, giving way to what appeared to be a level, expansive plain.

Ledyard and Drayton stared ahead, trying to make sense of what they faced when a pair of lights suddenly flashed far out in the darkness. Cocking his head, Ledyard heard the faint hum of an automobile engine.

It was the first of many vehicles, some alone, some in groups, passing back and forth on a major road. For half an hour Ledyard monitored the traffic, discovering to his dismay that the road was never free of travelers for more than sixty seconds.

His plan to use the road was no good, but he and Drayton would have to cross it just the same and that presented a new set of problems. They would have to sneak up, then dash across, not knowing what lay on the other side.

He knew he could not wait for daylight to reconnoiter. A wasted day would bring them nothing but consumption of what was left of the precious stores of water and food. Dawn might break at any moment. Ledyard clucked to the horse and they started forward.

The approach was agonizing. As the engine grew louder and the headlamps on the vehicles shone brighter, Ledyard's nerve wavered. The engines and lights repulsed him. They were man-made and he wanted nothing to do with them. Frantically, he thought of turning back. But to where? To what?

As they came closer, he altered the approach, halting when the lights flared, moving when they passed. He was amazed at Drayton. He seemed to know exactly what they were doing and after a few repetitions, he was starting and stopping on his own.

When they were near enough to see the partial bodies of the cars and trucks, Ledyard turned his attention to the road itself, scanning its edges as the lights swept past, looking for anything that might offer cover.

The light was too poor to see clearly but Ledyard thought he could discern the outline of a disabled truck among the indistinct hodge-podge of shapes strewn along the side of the roadway.

He waited several minutes until there was no traffic going in either direction, then moved forward at a fast trot. Suddenly, there were headlamps again. Ledyard and Drayton stopped immediately. A moment later a pool of faint light washed over them as the vehicle passed, apparently without seeing them.

Ledyard had gotten a clear look at the disabled truck. It was just ahead, heeled over at a good angle for concealment. What concerned him now was the suddenness with which the last lights had appeared. It could only mean that there was a curve or grade at this section of the highway and that was going to make the difficult crossing even trickier.

And there was something else. The smell of putrefied

flesh was in the air and it was making Drayton nervous. He was snorting, as if trying to clear the odor from his nose, and his anxious feet were dancing back and forth.

Cantering the last few yards to the deserted truck, Ledyard jumped down, maneuvered Drayton into the deepest shadows and huddled there with him. He pinched the horse's nostrils closed and stroked his neck as the lights of a dozen slow-moving vehicles bore down on them.

The convoy seemed to go on forever, and Ledyard's heart began to race when the last truck in line slowed, then veered toward the side of the road. "We've been spotted," he thought. But the driver was only reaching for a cigarette, and just as Ledyard was about to leave his hiding place, the vehicle picked up speed again and rolled down the road.

As he watched it rumble out of sight Ledyard thought he could detect the first, delicate streaks of dawn in the eastern sky.

Several more vehicles passed, taking with them five or six more minutes of time, enough to produce the first rosy harbingers of dawn.

He could wait no longer and with the whine of an engine approaching, he led Drayton up a small embankment and onto the still dark road.

Drayton snorted. He skittered to one side and then, as a pair of headlights pinned them in its oncoming beams, he rose high into the air, his hind feet clattering on the hard-packed road.

For Ledyard, everything happened in an instant. He saw the bodies of several dead horses piled on the side of the road, he saw the terror in Drayton's eyes and he saw the headlights closing in.

The vehicle was slowing rapidly and while he hung onto Drayton, Ledyard grabbed a grenade, pulled the pin and flung it in a straight line at the advancing lights.

He could see the grenade bouncing down the road and so did the driver. The big truck swerved wildly and went off the highway as the grenade exploded.

At the same time Ledyard grabbed a hunk of Drayton's mane and swung onto the terrified horse's back. They were plunging and rearing in the middle of the road as excited German voices rang out from the truck and new headlights converged from both directions.

Leaning low on Drayton's frothy neck, Ledyard gave him his head and screamed, "Go, boy, go!"

Drayton responded with a great bolt forward and, gathering his front legs in a frantic rush, soared over the dead horses.

Small arms fire sounded before they came to earth and bullets were singing in the air as they hit the ground running. Ledyard felt one skim across his hand. At the same moment the ground gave way and they were in water so deep that they went all the way under.

The impact knocked Ledyard to one side but he managed to grasp a handful of Drayton' s mane and was clinging to it when the horse broke water and began to swim, cutting through the water with long, powerful strokes.

The heavy pack kept dragging him under, and as Ledyard loosened it he lost his grip. Flailing blindly as Drayton's big body churned past he latched onto his tail and let himself be towed.

The heavy plop of bullets in water sounded all about them, but Drayton never slowed nor did he change direction, and they swam out of rifle range.

Ledyard lost his grip again as Drayton climbed out of the lake's muddy shallows. He sputtered to his knees, crawling through the muddy water until he gained the bank. There he lay gasping for a few seconds, then looked up to see Drayton shaking himself dry. He glanced back and saw that the lake they had crossed, though not wide, was exceedingly long. He could make out many vehicles along the road and he could hear the pop of an occasional rifle but he could see no indication of pursuit.

Ahead of them lay immense, half-tended fields of grain, a flawed rug of yellow draped over a landscape of round, rolling ridges. Taking up the reins, he boosted himself onto Drayton's back and they galloped into the undulating sea of wheat, straight toward the rising sun.

For an hour they rode through one field after another without seeing anyone, even on the lonely, rutted tracks that intersected the croplands.

Ledyard had picked up fugitive habits and was constantly scanning the territory in front of him, the sky overhead and the ground left behind. But his recent avowal of service to beauty was no passing fancy either. It was now a part of him too, and as they rode into the growing light he found that he was just as involved in the splendor around him as he was in any external threat.

The ordinary sight of a bird in flight inspired him to think about its marvelous construction, how long it had lived or what adventures it had experienced. The earth being kicked up by Drayton's feet emitted eternal odors that prompted him to speculate on the wondrous qualities of soil not only as a miracle of fertility but as an enduring repository of life inextricably linked with death. He listened to the breaths that Drayton took and ruminated on the energy that was soaking the seat of his pants in the form of sweat. He mused about the line that Drayton had descended from and the mysterious components that must have gone into the making of such an animal.

He regarded himself too, wondering where his legs had come from and how his knees had been invented, how his eyes were made to roll in their sockets, how his audacious heart could beat so incessantly.

He had never given anything but passing consideration to things like this before, and as they rode toward the shade of a lone tree at the crest of a low hill he realized that by merely taking the time to contemplate beauty he was freeing himself from the worries of past and future. Beauty was forcing him to exist in the moment.

The more he lived in the present, the richer, fuller and longer his life seemed to be. His imagination raced with all kinds of exciting possibilities for new ways of seeing and being.

As they neared the top of the hill Drayton's breathing seemed more labored and Ledyard gave his neck a pat of encouragement.

It was only then he realized Drayton had been shot. Fortunately, the slug had passed cleanly through a fatty portion of Drayton's neck, close to the line of his mane.

Ledyard ripped a sleeve off his shirt and poured the last of his water into the French helmet, which, like Drayton Witt's binoculars, had somehow remained with him during the chaotic swim across the lake.

He soaked part of the sleeve in the helmet and let Drayton drink the rest while he did what he could with the wound. Blood had caked on both sides and when it was cleared away he saw that the hole had already begun to close. He couldn't detect much swelling and felt confident that, baring infection, the injury would be nothing to worry about.

But the superficial nature of the wound didn't assuage Ledyard's guilt. He told the horse how deeply sorry and ashamed he was. Drayton paid the apologies little mind, for he was already engaged in cropping grass, but that didn't make Ledyard feel any better. If the wound had been more serious, he might have ridden Drayton to death. How could he have been so self-absorbed to have failed to check the condition of the creature that meant the most to him?

He promised himself that from now on he would look him over every time they stopped.

The injury to Ledyard's hand was not serious but it still stung, so he ran his tongue over the split skin, a faint move that Drayton noticed. Uncommonly aware, he often looked up from his feeding, but this time Ledyard was shocked to see an undeniable look of recognition in the horse's eyes.

Drayton turned purposefully and walked straight to where Ledyard was sitting, lowering his nose to the wounded hand. Ledyard lifted it slightly and Drayton sniffed. He could feel the moist air from the horse's lungs as his nostrils explored the line of the cut.

"It's not much," Ledyard whispered, "no purple heart for this."

To Ledyard's astonishment, Drayton's great tongue suddenly rolled out of his mouth and licked at the blood-caked line along the back of Ledyard's hand. It wasn't unusual for a horse to lick the salt from a man's hand, but never in Ledyard's experience had an animal licked him with such obvious intent. Drayton knew exactly what he was doing, and as he turned away to continue his grazing

Ledyard stared after him in open-mouthed wonder.

For several minutes he watched the horse carefully, trying to make a mental record of his every detail. If anything happened to him he wanted to remember Drayton always.

The little zephyrs blowing up the hill had built to a cooling breeze, and after rubbing a few flakes of debris out of his eyes, Ledyard rose up and took a look around.

It was a good vantage point, the highest for miles. He followed the hollow beat of artillery and saw faraway columns of smoke twisting into the sky.

Sighting through the field glasses he ascertained that the arising funnels of smoke were stacked one in front of the other and reasoned that the front was wide and the fighting hard.

Turning in the opposite direction he was able to make out what was left of two hamlets. As far as he could tell, both villages had been destroyed, for all that remained were the charred dregs of prominent buildings, jutting into the air like bones.

At the limit of the binoculars' range he saw hills covered with what looked like neat lines of fencing. That direction offered the least resistance and the most hope and that's the way they headed.

For the rest of the morning, they passed through semi-fallow fields without incident, and by early afternoon they were standing at the base of a hill that marked the beginning of a sprawling vineyard.

Row upon row of neglected vines marched up the slope, and in contemplating them Ledyard found his judgments jumping back and forth between pity and acceptance.

The vines were pitiful in the sense that they had been deserted. From the look of them, Ledyard figured they had received no attention in months, maybe years. They rested in untilled, hard-packed soil, which was dry and riddled with cracks. Many of the vines appeared dead. The best of them showed only the feeblest signs of life – a sprig of green stretching for the sun, a stunted, wilting leaf gasping for life.

Aside from a few faint cart tracks imbedded in the brittle ground there was no sign of man. There was no sign of shelling either but the wholesale neglect of what must have been a magnificent farm left Ledyard thinking that this was a prime example of how the tentacles of war insinuated themselves far beyond the battlefield.

The vineyard had not been touched directly but it had been ruined by war just the same, and he wondered how many of those who had cared for the vines, grunting and sweating and laughing under the sun, were now dead or displaced. "Just about all of them," he thought.

But while there was much to lament here, there seemed just as much to celebrate. Left to fend for itself, the vineyard was also free of the fussy hands of man, the same hands that created all the wars of the world. The vines were free to grow in any way they wanted, free to test themselves against natural elements, free to flourish or wither depending on their individual strengths or weaknesses. There was a great deal to be said for that way of being, and Ledyard imagined for a moment that the vineyard might be greater were it left to determine its own fate, growing wild and unfettered.

Drayton loved to attack inclines, and he tugged impatiently at the metal in his mouth as they started up the slope. But Ledyard held him back. They were both thirsty and the bullet hole in his neck had to have drained some of his resources.

Drayton settled down and as they rode higher on the hill, picking their way between the rows of vines, they discovered a few which, despite lack of attention, had done well enough to fill out their tendrils with broad, green leaves.

Peeking under the boughs Ledyard found several bunches of fat, succulent fruit. Cradling the treasure in his hand, he led Drayton even higher, stopping to rest in the shade of the biggest vine he could find.

There they picnicked, Drayton nibbling at the best of the leaves while Ledyard sat beneath him, popping the big, red grapes into his mouth with the relish of a child gobbling gumdrops.

The meaty moisture of the grapes had not slaked Ledyard's thirst when he rose out of the shade. The horse had begun to behave impatiently again, and Ledyard thought it might be because he smelled water. He was bobbing his head and swinging it from side to side, pausing every few seconds to stare at the crest of the hill.

Ledyard patted his chest and talked to him in soothing tones, but Drayton would not take his eyes off the brow of the hill. When Ledyard jumped onto his back, Drayton moved off at an eager walk. He insisted on dancing in place when Ledyard tried to hold him and, tiring of the tug of war, Ledyard gave him his head and Drayton surged into a gallop.

The breeze was in their faces as they surmounted the last of the rise. At the end of one vine row Ledyard could see something man-made. It was an old cistern built of rock. With a whoop of excitement he hurried Drayton on, images of fresh, clear water swimming through his head.

He did not see the motorcycle lying in the grass behind the old well. Nor did he see the German soldier standing behind the rock bound cistern, his face pressed against the surface of the water.

Ledyard saw nothing until it was too late and what he saw then, the dripping, startled face of a young soldier, sent his heart into his throat and Drayton into the air. Ledyard slid straight off Drayton's sweat-slicked back and sprawled in the dirt, practically at the German's feet.

For an instant the two young soldiers were unable to move. Then the German twisted his head at the motorcycle and Ledyard saw what he saw. A cartridge belt and pistol were coiled about the handlebars.

The German took a sudden step toward the motorcycle and Ledyard cried out:

"Wait!"

The German froze at the sound of the strange word and Ledyard jumped to his feet. In a gesture of peace he held out a hand, palm up.

"I won't hurt you," Ledyard said.

He patted his hips and threw up his hands. "I have nothing . . . you see . . . I have nothing."

He waved his arms briefly as a sign of disarmament. "English?" he asked.

Using his fingers to pull imaginary words from his lips, he repeated the word.

"English?"

The German seemed perplexed. He glanced once more at his gun and then at his surroundings as if to see if anyone was watching or listening. Then he made a few negative jerks with his head.

Shyly, the enemy soldier asked, "German?" and it was Ledyard's turn to shake his head.

Awkwardly, the youths stood their ground in silence and in those few moments of indecision Ledyard realized that his designated adversary was a real boy, a teenager even younger than himself. His heavy, straw-colored hair barely moved in the breeze and his rosy cheeks and pouty, red lips still carried the blush of extreme youth. At a distance he might have blended in as a man of war, but up close the tall boots and grown-up uniform and intense boyishness of his face made him look like part of an after-school charade.

"Is there water?" Ledyard asked, pointing at the cistern. "Water."

The German looked down at the well, then back at Ledyard. There certainly was nothing threatening about him. The tall flaxen haired youth looked frail, a hat rack of skin and bone. His uniform shirt was missing a sleeve and one of his leggings was gone. The rest of his outfit was in tatters.

There was no malevolence in his expression and his attitude suggested nothing that indicated a trained killer. He looked like a stray dog. "A stray dog with a horse," the German thought.

Still wary, he took a calculated step backward and flicked his fingers at the little reservoir.

Ledyard was wary too. He wanted to stay alert in case the stranger made a move toward the pistol. Deliberately, he picked up one of Drayton's reins and led him to the lip of the cistern. They stuck their heads in together and drank. The water was cold and delicious. He kept his eyes up, watching the German while he thought all the while, "Water is the best drink in the world."

Ledyard looked up from the well, and swiping the excess water from his mouth, smiled humbly at the German.

"Thank you . . . thank you for letting me drink."

The German nodded solemnly, and Ledyard stuck his head back in the well. When he could ingest no more, Ledyard pulled Drayton's head out too and offered his hand to the enemy.

"Thank you again."

The German regarded the outstretched hand with caution, then sent out his own and the two soldiers shook.

This simple, common action had a profound effect, for as their hands came together, the intimacy of flesh upon flesh dissolved the concept of enemy. Suddenly, the irrational need to kill each other was gone.

Drayton wanted more water. Ledyard fed out the rein and as the horse lowered his head into the tank the German took a step toward the animal.

"I like horses," he said, nodding toward Drayton.

"You can pat him, he's very gentle."

Ledyard took a small step back. "Go ahead."

Laying a hand on Drayton's neck, the German smiled back at Ledyard and said again, "I like horses."

The German felt along the length of the horse's body, around his rump and back to his neck. His hands were confident and Ledyard could tell that he was experienced.

As the German gave his neck a few final strokes Drayton pulled out of the water, licked his lips, shook himself and emitted a ludicrously long sigh of contentment.

Spontaneously, both men shared a laugh and, as they

did, a barrage of artillery fire began its hollow booming far away at the front. They listened to the reminder of war.

Wistfully, the German turned back to Drayton and caressed his shoulder. Then, he looked again at the sound of the artillery, and Ledyard could see that a thought was turning in his mind.

Nodding toward Drayton the German said, "Horses don't belong in war. It's no good."

The German gazed in the direction of the artillery and shook his head. "The war is no good. It's crazy."

Ledyard knew exactly what he was saying without understanding a single word.

"Absolutely insane," he agreed.

The two soldiers stood face to face in the vineyard. Each contemplated the ground at their feet for a few seconds and when they looked into one another's eyes again they were each thinking the same thing. The encounter had run its course and there was nothing left to do but part.

This time the German's hand came out first. "Good luck," he said shaking.

"Good luck," Ledyard echoed. Righting the motorcycle, the German swung a leg over and settled into the seat. When Ledyard saw him pick the pistol and cartridge belt off the handlebars he thought, "Maybe he's going to shoot me now."

The German turned and smiled as he fastened the weapon around his waist. He slipped a set of goggles up from his neck and shimmied the edges until they were comfortable. Starting to pull on a pair of gloves he paused and sat still, gazing over the handlebars.

At last he turned in Ledyard's direction. "Are you hungry?" Ledyard had no idea what he was asking.

He stared back with a dumb expression. "Do you want something to eat?" the German said, this time popping a phantom morsel into his mouth. Ledyard made no move. It seemed inappropriate now, to approach the enemy while he was armed. He nodded almost imperceptibly.

The German rummaged through a pouch that was slung across the gas tank. He brought out a flat, thick portion of bread and tossed it to Ledyard. Rifling deeper into the pouch he retrieved a tin of sardines and bounced them into the dirt at Ledyard's feet.

The German jumped on the kick-starter and the engine turned over. Teasing the accelerator, he waited as the motorcycle percolated into an even rhythm. Then he raised a gloved hand in farewell and started down the hill.

As Ledyard stooped to pick up the sardines he tried to sort through a jumble of thought and emotion. The solitary motorcyclist fading in the distance was a complex vision; the enemy, the kind stranger, the young man so much like him, the speaker of an alien language.

It was sad to see him go. Ledyard sat down in the dirt. He didn't know one thing in the whole world.

"There is lost," he said to himself. "And there is lost. Right now I am really, really lost."

Determined now to concentrate wholly on his feast, Ledyard set to the business of eating. He laid out his shirt as a tablecloth and opened the sardine tin with care. He placed the bread and the tin on his shirt and ate slowly.

When he was finished he had not spilled a drop of fish oil. Nor had he let the tiniest crumb escape. He stuck his head back in the cistern and drank until his stomach was bursting.

With the breeze at his back, he took in the long view of

the way he had come. The same way the German had gone. He decided the chances were no better than fifty-fifty that the kindly stranger might suffer a pang of conscience and report his existence to the first authority he came across. Maybe he wouldn't. Anyway, it didn't matter. He couldn't stay where he was.

Drayton's face was buried in the cistern as Ledyard picked up the reins.

"C'mon my friend, you're gonna be too waterlogged to walk. Besides," he said when he had swung onto Drayton's back, "we can't be late for the war. How would that look?"

THE WOMAN ON THE ROOF

For days she had performed the same afternoon ritual. Emerging after the sun was starting down she made her way around the side of the house to start the long climb toward the roof on a high wooden ladder. Then she would crawl across the red tiles until she reached a kind of parapet, a seat that afforded a view of the old barn a quarter of a mile away and the open country beyond.

But she did not come to admire the view. Each afternoon's performance was carried out with the same grim intention. She wanted to end her life in one graceful dive from the roof to a ribbon of concrete fifty feet below.

Until now she had been stymied in her quest by a plethora of distractions. The distractions themselves were not the problem. It was her unnecessarily addled mind. Her mind, which she knew was no longer in proper working order, could not resist sifting through trivial concerns. It was effectively blocking her goal and it often occurred to her that the struggle to die was keeping her alive.

The ridiculous aspects of the situation often made her smile for the woman on the roof possessed a keen intellect, keen enough to appreciate the subtlety, depth and complexity of human existence.

She had considered hanging, but had fretted over the mechanism so long that she dropped the idea in exasperation. Slitting her wrists had seemed a good idea but the pain of incision, the thought of slicing through the various layers of her own flesh and the fear of having second thoughts, at which time she would simply bandage up the wounds, drove her away from that idea. For a time she considered using a gun. But she would have to procure one, a process which seemed so complicated that she was unable to conjure a way even to begin. Besides, she had been plagued throughout her life with a fear of firearms.

The roof seemed the best way. One step into space and the deed would be done. That's what she had naively thought. But the roof had provided more barriers than she ever could have imagined. The onset of vertigo aborted her initial attempts to climb the ladder. It took two more days of negotiating the slippery roof tiles to reach the parapet and when she did she was too exhausted to jump.

Once the Germans came while she was crawling over the tiles and she shivered atop the house until they left. By that time it was long after dark. The night was moonless and she crawled inch-by-inch back to the ladder, a journey that seemed to take hours. When her toes finally touched ground, day was breaking.

The next afternoon was rainy as was the day after. She made a try on the second day anyway for the rain had begun to tail off but found the ledge of the parapet too slick for standing.

To a detached observer it might have seemed that the woman on the roof was insincere. It was true that many of the delays in reaching her sad aim had been brought on by herself, and it was also true that many of them seemed irrelevant when weighed against the gravity of her purpose.

But, if anything, she had been too sincere. Her determination was so deep and abiding that it could not tolerate failure in any form. This, coupled with a thoroughly distraught mental condition, had conspired against her unshakable desire to snuff out her pointless life.

She had now reached a point that put her in reach of the goal. The ladder had been mastered and she fairly scampered over the tiles. She would certainly have gone over the day before were it not for some eleventh hour difficulties with the dive itself. She wanted it to be foolproof and it was only after she had gained the parapet that she began to ponder what might happen if the trajectory was off.

She had counted on making a head-first landing and had often visualized her skull splitting on an impact of such force that her brains would explode upward.

But as she stood on the parapet it occurred to her that since she had never made such a dive how could she be sure it would have the desired effect?

What if she missed the walkway and broke her back or landed feet first and shattered her legs? What would she do then? Lay next to the house and starve in excruciating pain? Would some soldier happen by and put her out of her misery? What if the bullet lodged in her brain without killing her? What if someone from the village stopped in and managed to get her to some medical facility? What if the doctor managed to salvage what was left of her, just enough to keep her in a chair being spoon-fed for the rest of her life?

The possibilities were so endless and so unremittingly

dreary that she had broken down as she stood on the parapet.

If only she were not a woman alone. If only there was someone standing below pleading with her not to do it she could have jumped easily. She could not depend on herself, and she had left the roof the evening before feeling thoroughly defeated. But she lay in bed that night, gazing at the patterns inside her closed eyes and told herself that if she just kept trying, sooner or later she was bound to succeed.

The next afternoon she stood on the parapet dressed only in a sculptor's smock and high button shoes. She felt certain that the time had finally come. She no longer worried about angles or ladders or Germans or villagers. Her mind was perfectly clear and if it had not been for the breeze she surely would have plunged to her death.

She had not noticed the lively currents until she was balanced on the ledge. The breeze was extraordinarily cool for the time of year and as she brought her hands together in the manner of a swimmer, a gust of it blew the smock up, exposing her from the waist down.

Reflexively, she pushed the material down along the front of her legs. But as she held the smock down the light, incessant wind eddied around her ankles, stole up her thighs and caressed the place where her legs met.

Her skin tingled and flashed as a wave of longing broke over her and she found her thoughts tumbling in a free fall of surrender and rapture and pure carnal lust.

She braced herself in the midst of the curious spasm and with great effort brought herself back to the need for death. A calm descended on her and, taking a deep breath, her eyes opened for a last look at the world.

A man in uniform was leading a horse up to the barn.

A COUPLING

Ledyard had spotted the buildings from afar. They were sequestered in groves of tall trees and with the binoculars he had been able to see pieces of them clearly.

The nearest structure seemed to be a barn or storehouse of some kind. There were two shell holes in the roof and a portion of one stone side bore a gaping hole that began at the eaves and extended half way to the foundation. A few of the surrounding trees had also been destroyed, but as far as he could tell the place was reasonably intact.

Beyond the barn, parts of a large, two-story house were visible. It, too, was surrounded by tall trees and, like the barn, had been wounded by shellfire.

He could see no signs of habitation outside either structure but the fact that they were both standing in war-torn country made him uneasy. Any standing structure was likely to be in use.

Ledyard dearly wanted a night out of the open and, after thirty minutes of careful watching, during which time no flash of movement had been seen, he decided to gamble.

As they crossed the last open ground, a field overgrown with weeds and large patches of wild wheat, he remained on Drayton's back. Riding bareback for so long had chaffed his buttocks raw and no amount of shifting gave relief. His legs ached constantly and the taut muscles in the small of his back throbbed with every step.

He knew that Drayton's spine was just as sore, but he dared not get down. If they were surprised while he was on the ground, any slim chance for escape would be lost.

The stiff breeze was in his face, a condition that favored their approach. If anyone was about, it would be difficult to hear the coming of a horse. Conversely, any sound from the house or barn would be easy to detect.

When they reached the trees that circled the barn, Ledyard stopped and listened. The wind was passing through the branches overhead and the noisy rustle of a million leaves sounded like the muted roar of a high-running sea. He listened hard for several minutes but could hear only the sounds made by the wind.

Holding onto Drayton's neck with both hands he dropped onto the ground and started stiffly toward the barn. He paused again when he reached one of its sides. Peeking around the corner he could see the stately old mansion several hundred yards away. The trees around it were bending this way and that in the swirling wind, making the stillness of the place more pronounced.

He watched the windows but nothing moved behind them. He covered the long path that wound through the trees between the house and the barn but, aside from lines of dead leaves skipping along in the gale, nothing moved there either.

The ground immediately in front of the barn was unkempt but open. The large wooden door marking the entrance was ajar, its latch lying broken on the ground. On the far side of the barn, partially obscured by overgrowth, was the base of a well with a hand pump growing out of it.

Ledyard made one last inspection of the deserted space and led Drayton across to the pump. He gripped the handle and depressed it. As he had feared, it made a loud, grating squeak. He waited and listened. There was no new sound on the wind.

He pumped rapidly and, after several screeching strokes, water began to gush from the faucet.

He filled the helmet several times and when they had finished drinking he stepped to the head of the trail and looked up the lonely path leading to the house. There was no sign of life and, confident that they were alone, he walked back across the open space, put his shoulder against the massive door and led Drayton into the barn.

The interior was a still life of destruction. Pieces of the splintered roof were scattered over the floor where they had fallen. In a far corner a portion of one wall had collapsed, creating a tall mound of mortar and stone piled in a heap like the tailings of a mine.

Farm tools and horse harnesses and dozens of other miscellaneous items had been left hanging from pegs on the rock walls and wooden beams. A store of grain sacks, gutted by mice and rats, were stacked under a low loft that still held the mowings of a hay harvest long past.

In a blackened pile of rubbish on the floor Ledyard found ration tins with German lettering. Judging from the thick layer of dust on the discarded containers the enemy had been absent for a long time.

Brightening the gloomy old barn were the beating wings and rackety chirping of scores of small birds who had made the ruin their exclusive domain. Some danced about their nests on high rafters while others zoomed in and out of the great tears in the roof, displaying their amazing aerial dexterity.

As lodging, the abandoned barn was a palace compared to what he had lately endured and, after seeing to Drayton's bullet wound, Ledyard went to work. In an hour's time he cleared a large portion of the floor. Then he scaled the loft and pushed enough dusty hay over the edge to cover most of the open area below.

By the time he dropped back down Drayton was already standing on the fresh carpet of old wheat, pawing at it with one hoof. He circled, went to his knees and lay down with a loud, unabashed groan. Then he rolled back and forth in ecstasy, shut his eyes with a sigh and fell into a snoring sleep. Wanting a nap himself Ledyard lay down with his back against Drayton's.

But he could not drift off, and when he saw a scythe leaning against one of the walls he decided to go out and cut the horse some grass while there was still light.

Shouldering the sickle, Ledyard walked to the door and was about to open it wider when he had second thoughts. Instead he peeked cautiously around the door to make sure that no one was in the vicinity.

Someone was lying face-up on the ground not six feet from the barn's entrance. It was a woman wearing only a shift and a pair of shoes. She seemed to be asleep but Ledyard was sure that she was wounded or ill.

Of course she was neither, for the woman on the ground had placed herself there on purpose. She had watched Ledyard the entire time he had been in the barn and when he started out she had seen her chance and dashed around to the front.

Ledyard went to one knee and looked down into a face that was extraordinarily beautiful. The bangs of her short, thick hair cut across a broad forehead anchored by pronounced brows. Her eyes were large and even the lids which covered them looked pretty. She had a well-formed nose and large, beautifully proportioned lips which were so inviting that Ledyard wondered in passing what it would be like to kiss them.

The woman's color was good and, looking up and down her body, he could see no blood. The rise and fall of breath was steady and the expression on her face was serene.

Ledyard ran his fingertips along one of her cheeks and recoiled as the lids of her eyes flew open. He thought he was gazing down at an angel.

She thought much the same. The boy above, with his hair the color of grass and gray eyes and gentle, open face had given her hope as soon as she had seen him. Perhaps the gaunt young man in the odd uniform had come to save her from fate. Perhaps he would stay with her and over time be able to fill the unfillable void inside her.

To Ledyard's surprise, the woman on the ground took his hand in one of hers and pressed it deep against her cheek. Her eyes remained focused on his and her lips parted slightly and spread into a subtle, dreamy smile.

"I wanted to make sure you had no evil intent," she whispered in French. "I know you don't."

The sound of her voice impressed Ledyard as having an ethereal, almost dream-like quality, and for an instant he wondered if he might be experiencing an hallucination brought on by lack of food. Not knowing one word of French he responded by pointing at himself and saying:

"American . . . I'm American."

It was the only thing he could think of to say, and as soon as the words were out of his mouth he felt foolish for having uttered them. What difference did it make if he was American? It told nothing about him but his nationality.

He half expected the woman on the ground to laugh at his ridiculousness but instead her soft eyes grew even warmer.

"American," she repeated.

She started to rise and Ledyard jumped to his feet and offered a hand.

When she was up the woman bewildered Ledyard by pressing in against him with a strange familiarity. She laid the side of her face softly against his chest and ran her hands briefly around his back. With a sign of satisfaction she began to caress the sides of his torso with her fingertips, drawing back when she felt the prominence of his ribs.

With a look of concern she gazed up at him. "You're starving."

"I don't understand," he said feebly.

"Hungry . . . are you hungry? Do you want food?" She used the same universal signs the German at the cistern had made, and for a moment Ledyard thought he was living some strange, recurring dream in which everyone he met asked the same question. But he managed to nod in the affirmative, and when he did the woman's eyes brightened.

"I'll get you something," she said, stepping backwards. "Stay here. I'll be back in a few minutes. Don't go anywhere. I'll come right back and I'll feed you."

With that she turned and hurried up the path leading to the house, her billowing smock revealing a set of sturdy shapely legs.

He understood that she was going for food, but who she was and why she was behaving so oddly was a mystery. She was acting as if he were an intimate, a relative or a former lover, yet he knew that was impossible. Or was it? Had she known an American that looked like him? No, it couldn't be.

He picked up the scythe and started toward the fallow field just below the barn. "Everything is a mystery," he thought, pausing to strip off the stinking, sleeveless rag he had worn for so long as a shirt. He dropped it into the grass wishing he would never have to look at it again much less wear it. He decided to get out of his boots too. He wished he didn't have to see them again either.

The wind had died and what was left of the sun felt wonderful on his shoulders. He'd never used a scythe, and it took some time to figure it out. Once he got the hang of wielding the long blade he was amazed at how the wheat fell before it.

To work in open air and sunshine and to feel honest sweat dripping down his face and chest was a tonic. For a few minutes he was able to forget about everything except what he was doing. The far-away thump of artillery was even forgotten as the scythe moved from side to side, and the aroma of fresh-cut grass went to his head.

Feeling slightly faint, he was about to quit when he heard her call. She was standing near the barn, one arm upraised. He lifted an arm in response and she turned away, walking casually in the direction of the barn.

As he stopped to gather up as much of the mowing as he could carry, Ledyard again found himself unable to imagine what her presence meant.

She was sitting on a drop cloth under a low, cozy tree, slathering preserves from a ceramic jar on a hunk of bread. When she heard him come up she glanced over her shoulder and gave him an easy smile. She patted the edge of the cloth, inviting him to sit next to her.

"Wait just a minute," he said, tipping his head toward the barn. "I have to feed my horse . . ."

He dumped the wheat in his arms near the barn door, stuck his head through the dark opening and called. A moment later Drayton walked sleepily into the light of late afternoon. Ledyard spread the new grass around with his bare toe. Drayton's nose dropped straight to the cuttings, and he began to feast.

A sudden fit of shyness seized Ledyard as he returned to the picnic site. She was pouring wine into glass tumblers and glanced up with another fetching smile but Ledyard found sitting down awkward. He was half-naked and barefoot and didn't know what to say or how to say it.

He stood over the drop cloth like a young man calling on someone for the first time.

She seemed to know how he felt. Her lips spread slowly in another radiant smile and she tugged sweetly at his pant leg.

Reassured, Ledyard sat down and began to gnaw at the jam-covered bread she handed him. Nothing had ever tasted so good and no table had ever looked so sumptuous. There was cheese and fruit and a whole basket of bread. A smaller basket held a large bottle of wine.

Off to one side was a large wash pan with some folded clothes and a bar of soap. He was lost in trying to figure out what it was for when she nudged his arm and handed him a half-full tumbler.

"To your health," she said, clinking her glass against his.

"Cheers," Ledyard replied.

He had never been much of a drinker and took a petite sip. The wine was harsh and acidic as it went down. He was amazed to see the woman sitting next to him take several long swallows without stopping. Her eyes met his over the lip of her glass, and Ledyard was prompted once more to wonder if they had ever met. She looked so content.

They didn't try to talk much as they ate. Ledyard said "thank you" over and over. The woman in the smock spoke only a rare word or two. Most of the time she seemed happy to watch him eat.

The woman on the roof was deeply grateful that fate had sent such a pleasant, good-looking young man to relieve her. Being in his company shut out the past completely, and halfway through the repast she realized to her joy that she could no longer remember her name. Nor could she remember the details of her life up to this moment. There was no recollection of the man she had married or the children she had given birth to. She was free of all memory of war as well, the merciless war which had ripped away everything she held dear and left her to suffocate in loneliness.

The woman knew only that she was riding the crest of the thrilling wave known as love. She could hardly bear to look at the emaciated young American sitting next to her, for each time she saw his face she wanted to touch him. Like all lovers she dreaded the first kiss, fearing it might not be returned, but she trusted that at some point the desire which dominated her every thought would overrun her fear.

She had wanted to give herself to him almost from the moment she had seen him leading the horse up to the barn. But she had waited as she was waiting now, hoping they would come together at just the right moment, effortless and without words.

For different reasons Ledyard was also waiting. From one moment to the next he had no idea how to proceed. He had difficulty looking at her because he did not know what to say. He could not move because he didn't know what to do. And he didn't know what to think because he didn't have any sense of how to be.

Ironically, his befuddlement did nothing to lessen the charge growing in the atmosphere around them. His boyishness perfectly suited the ambiance of emerging love and that same intense timidity had the effect of driving the sublime tension residing under the tree to even greater heights.

Though he did not comprehend what was happening, Ledyard could certainly feel it. The more wine he drank the easier it went down. But the pleasing inebriation that crept in on him did not muddy his thoughts at all. The warm, lazy feeling the wine produced seemed to make his thinking clearer, and as he filled his stomach his mind filled with images of her.

She was attractive in every aspect it seemed. The color of her skin, the curve of her neck, the shape of her mouth, the contours of her nose, even the thickness of her calves was pleasing.

But her physical qualities were surpassed in Ledyard's mind by her way of being. She seemed remarkably free and assured of herself down to the tiniest gesture and these attributes made Ledyard's intoxication complete. His attraction was sealed when she reached in front of him for the wine bottle, passing an arm close enough to smell her skin. As soon as the odor traveled up his nose he realized that it was an aroma he could inhale over and over without losing its appeal.

When she was sated with food and drink the French woman stretched out on the drop cloth, shielding her eyes from the sun with the back of a hand. A few moments later she took her hand away and squinted at Ledyard who was still stuffing bread into his mouth.

"I can't stop," he said sheepishly.

The woman smiled knowingly and rolled onto her stomach to doze, using her folded arms for a pillow. Spreading her legs slightly, she squirmed against the earth and, as she did the flimsy garment covering her was hiked to mid-thigh.

Ledyard's reserve began to melt at the sight of her and, with that barrier removed, he let his mind run loose. He wondered how it would be to touch her thigh with his hand and if she would spread her legs wider if he did. He imagined his groin pressed against the smooth, plump curve of her rump and if she would pull the fabric covering higher if he did. He pictured his face burying itself in the nape of her neck and how it would be to drink in the essence of her. He could barely stand to look at her now because in every spot he trained his eyes, whether it was the sole of her shoe or the lobe of her ear, he saw an object of desire.

If he had touched her at that moment it is likely she would have responded with a fervor beyond his dreams. But instead of touching her he turned away and looked for Drayton.

The horse had tired of his feast and had drifted a few yards away from the barn to try his luck with what was growing wild. Ledyard wondered if he should get up and give him some water but decided not to. He wanted to stay right where he was. He wanted to savor every moment of his marvelous satisfaction.

Grasping it by the neck, he lifted the bottle of wine to his lips and took a last mighty swig. Lowering it, he glimpsed at the sleeping woman once more.

Her shoulder was rising and falling with the uniform timing of sleep, but as he watched her slumber it occurred to him, though he knew nothing about her feelings or thoughts or likes or dislikes, that she was human, a separate entity that might as well have been the only one beside himself on earth.

She was alone and complete and somehow miraculous and Ledyard realized that the simple existence of her humanity was at the root of his longing. It was the springboard from which his desire had been launched.

At that moment he knew that he loved her. It didn't matter if he touched her, and whether or not she responded was suddenly of little concern. He could feel her humanity, it was precious to him, and secure in that knowledge, Ledyard lay back himself. The meal was churning agreeably in his stomach and as he stared at the twilight filtering through the branches overhead he fell into a little sleep of his own.

He was floating dreamily in a half-sleep when he felt her mouth hovering over his own. He felt the sensuous press of her lips and opened his eyes. Her sleepy, smiling face was peering down at him. Without any urgency she lowered her mouth to his and they kissed as if it was for the thousandth time instead of the first. Then she lifted her face, gave him a lazy grin, and got to her feet, helping him up in the process.

She picked up the washbasin standing nearby, slipped an arm around his waist and led him to the pump at the edge of the clearing in front of the barn. She placed the tub on the ground and faced him.

"Take your pants off," she said.

"What?"

"Take your pants off," she repeated sweetly.

Ledyard laughed shyly. "What?" he said again. With a coy look of exasperation she sat down and quickly unlaced her shoes. Then she jumped up barefoot, grabbed the hem of her frock in each hand, pulled it over her head and tossed it to one side.

She said the words once more, scolding him playfully. "Take off you pants . . . I want to have a bath with you." Ledyard's first instinct was to turn and run. Though he had always coveted girls and had pursued a number of them as a teenager, a woman had never stood naked before him.

The girl he had remembered in the sloop on Lake Michigan had been his most intimate lover. Their tongues had spent hours together and on two occasions he had held her breasts fully in his hands.

Together with a few boyhood chums he had made a spontaneous visit to a house of ill repute in Grand Rapids. His romantic ideals however, had chased him from the house at the last minute and he had spent the evening leaning against a lamppost outside, smoking cigarettes as he waited for his friends.

Ledyard could barely look at the woman standing in front of him but an intangible, unbreakable trust that he felt toward the stranger made him stand his ground.

The shock on his face must have been monumental, because the French woman laughed out loud when she looked at him.

Before he could react her arms were around his neck and he could feel the soft crush of her breasts against his bare chest. Her lips brushed against his cheeks and she stared into his eyes.

"My sweet man," she said softly.

Then she quickly undid his trousers, pulled them over his hips with a series of quick, sexless jerks and turned away. She was pumping water into the washbasin by the time Ledyard stepped out of his pants.

Too shy to move, he stood still in the fading light, knowing that something was going to happen. Though he knew what the something was, he didn't dare to visualize it. Nor could he imagine how he would get from where he now stood to the kind of intimacy he knew was coming.

The adrenaline of anticipation was rising in him and as it did a curious calm began to assert itself. With each passing moment the constraints of awkwardness were falling further and further away.

As he was watching her tear a ragged cloth in half he realized that it was useless to think. He had been swept into a current with powers that made his own seem puny and the less he struggled the better he felt. He was giving up, and it produced a sensation that made him feel lighter than air, a sensation so exquisitely exciting that he wanted it to last forever.

He had vowed to live in the moment without fully comprehending what that meant but now he knew.

Like Ledyard, the woman at the pump was in the grip

of something she knew was vastly more powerful than her. And like him, she too was nervous with anticipation.

As she worked a lather into the torn cloth she thought she might be consumed by fire at any moment. Flames were scampering through her scalp. They were dancing across her breasts, rippling along her spine and pricking her buttocks. They were licking up between her legs, and every thought was focused on quenching them. The desire to touch herself was surpassed only by the desire to be touched by him, and she pumped the water, tore the cloth and lathered the soap in a feverish attempt to forestall her need.

None of these things showed on her face as she placed the basin at his feet. She smiled at him sweetly, pressed a hunk of soap and a piece of cloth into one of his hands, turned him around and began to scrub his shoulders. She had thought that feeling his skin with her fingers would provide a measure of relief but, if anything, touching his skin made her desire more real.

Ledyard was only going through the motions of washing himself. His concentration was trained solely on the unfamiliar hands working their way down his back and when he felt the washcloth dive into the crevice between the cheeks of his behind he gave a little start and dropped his soap.

She rubbed the cloth up and down both his legs and, revolving easily around him, dumped the water from the basin slowly over his head. Wanting the smell of her on him, she picked the smock off the ground and made signs that he should dry off with it.

Then she went back to the pump, refilled the basin and stood in front of him again with a smile.

"My turn," she said, offering her back.

Ledyard stood poised with the cloth and soap, frozen in space. As he wondered how to proceed, his hand seemed to assume a life of its own and an instant later it was riding a bubbly film of soap across her square shoulders.

From the corner of his eyes he saw Drayton standing a few feet away, watching them curiously.

He loved the muscled curves of her back and the thought passed briefly through his head that he could do this all the time. When he reached the small of her back he hesitated. Looking down, he was at once excited and fearful of the cool white rise of her rump. Suddenly, a hand was touching his, guiding it gently into the flawless crack.

He began to rub up and down with the cloth and heard her moan. Her backside met the pressure of his hand with pressure of its own and all at once Ledyard was tumbling in a breathtaking dream.

The pristine nape of her neck drew his lips down and he kissed her lightly behind the ear. Her head was already turning to meet his as his mouth traveled along her jaw line. When his lips came to the corner of her mouth his excitement increased tenfold. All vestiges of restraint fell away.

Thinking was now impossible. The complexity of being human had been reduced to the rush of two mouths who had never known one another, coming together as if their whole lives had been destined for this moment.

In the coolness of twilight he tasted her warm breath and the wetness of her mouth. Each tactile probing, no matter how small, heaped more and more tinder on the fire that was racing through them. What might happen or even what would happen was lost in the thrill of having their arms go around each other. Nothing existed as they hurtled toward union, kissing harder and harder, holding each other with ever-increasing power in a fervent bid to make themselves into one.

They ran their hands anywhere they wanted, because without thought nothing was forbidden. He spread the folds of her behind as she took him in her hands, rubbing and stroking him frantically.

They dropped to the ground and climbing into one another's laps, their mouths locked in an ongoing kiss neither could bear to break off. They rolled onto their sides, entwining in an embrace that sought, by sheer force, to achieve a weld that could not be ruptured.

One of his legs slipped between hers and he felt intense heat. She threw herself against his thigh, opening all of herself to him and he could feel moisture spreading over his skin.

She pulled him over her and, throwing her legs wide, drew him down. Suddenly, without guidance or fumbling he was inside, swimming up into her. He plunged as far as he could go and still tried to go deeper. She encouraged him with great upward thrusts, pushing all of herself against him.

He wanted to split her in two and she wanted the same. Nothing mattered so long as they were coupled.

A gate opened, and, as she shrieked in ecstasy, he flooded inside her.

Ledyard hung over her a moment, staring down in exhausted shock at her open mouth as it sucked air. A drop of his sweat splashed softly on her cheek. He slumped against her and rolled onto the ground. They lay staring together at the darkness falling across the sky, both struggling to breathe.

After what seemed a long time Ledyard turned his head and found her looking straight at him with dreamy, half-closed eyes. He was amazed that anyone could look so serene. Making a short, happy sigh she gazed at the night sky and took some of his fingers in her own, holding them with unhurried pleasure.

Ledyard was unable to speak. He could not imagine looking at her again. He was afraid it would be some cruel dream of war, as disappointing and disillusioning as everything else. It was only when he heard her voice that he managed to look into her face. The whites of her eyes were shining as she stared at him.

"I'm going to the house," she said in the oddly, husky voice. "We should sleep out. We need blankets. I'll see if I can find some more wine."

She wanted to say more but was too tired for pantomiming explanations. She smiled her sweet smile and said, "Stay."

Touching him lightly with her fingertips she climbed shakily to her feet. "Stay," she said again, holding her palm out like a traffic policeman. "Stay here, I'll be back." Ledyard could hear her light footsteps on the path but did not turn to look. He lay still. It was unlikely that he would have behaved any differently had he understood every word. Wild showers of spark-like images were racing unchecked through his brain.

Sexually, he had been brought wide-awake in one spectacular stroke. He had never known what other people did, but whatever that might be it could in no way exceed the completeness he felt. He still could not grasp what had transpired. Disbelief and certainty were co-existing in his mind and the banging of one against the other was creating the enormous shower of sparks.

It wasn't the way he had pictured love between a man and a woman. Ledyard had dreamed that love would have a gossamer, ethereal quality. This had been muscle and sweat and lust and he was momentarily ashamed of what he had done, ashamed of his unseemly thoughts, especially the one about splitting her open.

But any doubt he might have harbored was overwhelmed by what he was feeling. His body was light and heavy. At one moment he was expecting to levitate while at the next it seemed he was sinking into the earth.

The unique odor of their sex was still in the air and he could feel liquid burning cold on his hip. He was trying to remember every picture of their coming together but new images, some carnal, some innocent, kept exploding the chronology.

Suddenly, he was chilly and when he turned to look up the vacant path he realized he was stiff in every muscle and bone. Teetering off balance, he gained his feet, grabbed up his clothes and hurried into the barn, hoping that Drayton was already there and he wouldn't have to go out looking for him.

Drayton was not only there but already down in the hay. His back was facing the door and he was snoring so contentedly that Ledyard thought better of getting him up for water. Instead, he pulled on his trousers and nestled in the hay a few feet away from the horse.

Coincidentally, he had made his bed directly under one of the ragged holes that opened in the roof forming a magnificent skylight.

Ledyard stared drowsily at the stars that had begun

to appear. Some were steady, some seemed to blink. For the first time he had the impression that the color of some were different from others . . . blue, white, silver, red. As he watched, he experienced the pleasant sensation of floating toward them. Or perhaps they were coming his way. He couldn't tell. They appeared as he watched, so many that he could not see each one as it became visible. Thousands of them were glittering when he fell asleep.

The perfect comfort of travel in a cold, black void astonished him. Somehow he remained in light as he glided effortlessly into the recesses of nowhere. He was not afraid, nor was he curious about what unknown power was fueling his journey. He was too warm to worry, bundled as he was in a cap and blanket, voyaging impervious through a zone of forbidding cold and emptiness.

He was well into the dream before he realized that Drayton was beneath him, a mass of muscle and sheen, surging through space with the same aplomb as his rider. Drayton was smiling and Ledyard knew at that moment that it was the horse who was powering him.

The stars came closer and closer lighting up the night. Ahead was what looked like a highway of stars, a great carpet of twinkling light stretching to infinity .

They were passing over the great bed of stars and Ledyard looked down to see that even though Drayton's hooves were not touching the road, great electrical sprays of light and color were being thrown up as they passed over. He looked back and saw an enormous rooster tail of the same material trailing behind him.

Though it came without discomfort of any kind he could feel heat building in both of them. The acceleration was fantastic and all at once they were melting sensuously into the millions of stars at their feet. Ledyard had never felt such ecstasy and as they dissolved into the luminous, eternal river below he opened his mouth and woke up.

The stars were poking through the crooked hole above him but he only saw them long enough to blink. The French woman's body was warm against his legs. Her head was at his waist, loving him with a deliberate, earnest desire.

For an instant Ledyard thought what she was doing and what she wanted him to do was crazy and the words "This is not right" sped through his mind. But they left just as quickly, for he was powerless in the face of her blissful determination.

Allowing himself a few moans of pleasure he dropped his head back into the hay, arched his back and let her take all of him.

She climbed up his torso, tenderly kissed his face several times and rolled onto her back.

They lay together like they had in the twilight and, after several moments Ledyard lifted a finger and pointed at the hole in the roof.

"Stars," he said. "Stars," she repeated in French.

A WORLD OF THEIR OWN

Ledyard woke wondering where he was. Dusty beams of sunlight had penetrated the holes in the roof and the birds were deep into their everyday chatter. Drayton was up and nibbling at the fringes of the hay that had been their bed.

When he looked at the sleeping woman Ledyard's internal compass began to spin. How could he be in love with someone he didn't know? Everything had happened so fast. He had not known what he was doing. He still did not know. Did she love him? Was she a dream? Would she go with him? How could that be accomplished? Would they keep on making love? Would she betray him to the enemy?

There were no answers to any of the questions. It made him uneasy, and in a panic he thought of making a getaway.

Yet, when he looked at her innocent form he knew that he was not going anywhere. Though not privy to the facts of her existence, he already knew what was important. She was kind and ravishingly beautiful and had given herself completely, holding nothing back. She knew what she wanted and Ledyard loved that. In his naive, untested notions of romance he had pined for someone who was feminine enough to sweep him off his feet and powerful enough to decide things for herself.

The woman lying next to him was the dream and to his amazement Ledyard found himself becoming aroused at the thought of how perfect she seemed. The smell of her body mixed with the musty smell of the hay fanned his passion and, as he lay propped on one elbow, he was tempted to reach over and caress her shoulder.

Drayton nickered lowly. He was standing next to the barn's closed door, nosing it impatiently, wanting to go out.

With a wistful look at the woman in the hay, Ledyard rose up and buttoned the front of his pants. His every muscle was stiff and he walked stilt-like to where Drayton was standing. Delightful thoughts swam through his head with every step and he found himself thinking, "I can't wait for her to wake up."

Drayton swung his face around as Ledyard came up and buried it in the crook of his arm, holding it very still in a display of sweet devotion that Ledyard acknowledged with a series of light, unhurried kisses.

The day was already very warm, and after Drayton had drunk what he needed from the basin, Ledyard slipped out of his trousers, refilled the tub and poured the cool contents over his head. He drank his fill from the faucet and sat a few moments on the pump stand letting the sun dry him.

The air was not moving, and he welcomed the promise of a lazy day. The birds seemed to have slowed their rhythm as they dawdled in the trees. Even the insects had a pronounced lethargy as they drifted slowly through the space in front of his face. It was still and peaceful as a Sunday back home.

Ledyard soon realized that the sound of artillery was missing. It had been so incessant since his arrival on the continent that its absence now seemed unnatural. He immediately thought that something dramatic might have happened. There might be a truce or the war might be over. It was wonderful to think that the orgy of destruction might have ceased.

The hollow, unmistakable boom of a big gun sounded in the distance. It was followed by more and more rumbles and in no time had settled into the dull, steady cadence he loathed. His hands went to his ears as he dropped his chin in the manner of one who is being tortured by sound.

When he lifted his eyes he saw Drayton in peace, carelessly swishing flies away with his tail as he grazed contentedly below the barn. And when he looked at the dark slit of the open door he knew that even if she was not yet awake, the woman inside was waiting for him.

He consoled himself with the thought that the war was still far away and, unable to wait any longer, picked up his pants and made for the cool interior of the barn.

She was on her back, gazing up at him with a sleepy, tender smile. They stared into one another's eyes for a long time and it struck Ledyard that they were making the same kind of love with their looks as they had with their bodies.

With a moan of pleasure she rolled onto her stomach and stretched out languidly. He had to touch her and passed his hand lightly over her back, his fingers tracing her bare skin in awe.

She writhed slightly at his touch, pressing her body deeper into the hay. Involuntarily, Ledyard lowered his face and felt the coolness of her skin with his lips.

As his kisses traveled up her spine she took the hand resting softly on her shoulder and slipped one of his fingers into her mouth, moving it slowly in and out.

By the time he had kissed his way to her shoulder she could feel the fullness of him against one of her legs. She twisted her head and their mouths fell together in a long, drenching kiss.

They pounded at each other insatiably, her moans increasing until she was echoing the action of her body with a frantic, breathless stream of unknown words and phrases.

For a long time she lay and he stood, the only sound being the sharp intake of their lungs. He dropped down and their sweat mingled as they lay half-entwined, listening to the undemanding sounds of the growing day.

In the delirious aftermath of a marvelous copulation, the lovers fell asleep.

It was toward noon when she woke. The sleep had been deep but she still felt tired and her first thoughts were of food. She did not consider the need to be connected with personal health or even pleasure. Food was merely the fuel they both needed for lovemaking. To be joined with him again had become her reason for being and though she no longer remembered the history of the house above the barn, or the role she might have played in it, the place represented the most likely source of food. She stole out of the barn and climbed the path in hope of finding some.

Ledyard woke twenty minutes later. Unlike his lover, he knew his own name and could easily have recalled the salient details of his personal history had he wanted. But the facts of his existence no longer seemed to carry weight either. In less than twenty-four hours, his life had assumed an entirely new and simplistic form.

He was an entity rooted quite happily in a patch of ground in Belgium, his sole companions consisting of a horse and a woman. All that his life demanded was that he care for the horse and love the woman, love her not as Ledyard Dixon but as a spirit in possession of the necessary equipment to practice love. Beliefs he might have held, complexities of the surrounding world, the fate of man, all of it had been rendered forgettable. All that mattered was seeing her again. And touching her.

Being alone had become intolerable and he left the barn frantic to find one of them. Shielding his eyes against the glare of noon he called for Drayton and was happy to see him appear almost immediately below the barn. Without encouragement he came straightaway, striding with the same kind of purpose an obedient child might use in answering a parent's call.

He watered him and rubbed him down with the old shirt going over Drayton's body with a thoroughness he had never used on anything. He knew that it would not be truthful to say that he worked so methodically out of love for Drayton alone. He took his time because there was a significant measure of shyness that still dogged him.

Part of what had happened was as frightening as it was exciting. He much preferred that she come to him and, as he worked on Drayton, he couldn't help glancing toward the path, expecting her to appear at any moment.

But when he had finished the path was still empty and he sat on the pump for minutes that grew longer and longer, wishing that he had a cigarette.

The house looked gloomy, even in the brightness of

midday and no amount of strained listening brought sound to his ears. The house remained still as a church. Too still.

Ledyard jumped on Drayton and when they neared the house he saw that it was in much poorer condition than he had thought. Great chunks of wall had been blown away and in several spots he could see through to the interior. No attempt had been made to repair shutters, most of which were hanging askew. Rain gutters were missing large sections, broken window glass had gone unreplaced and the roof's tiling was checker boarded with damage.

Turning a corner they followed a curving walkway to the front of the old house and found that it no longer existed. In its place was a gargantuan sprawl of wood and plaster and brick. The piles of plaster and brick rolled across the frontage in immense mounds, punctuated by wooden splinters of beams and rafters, which jutted everywhere, like pins in a cushion.

As he slid off Drayton he noticed that the long tree-bordered driveway also bore the scars of war. The once smooth drive was dotted with pockmarks.

At the center of the house was a well-trodden track and Ledyard followed it through tall cones of rubble, some of them higher than his head. He had penetrated deep into the house before the first ruined rooms came into view.

There was a hallway that looked intact, though he had to step up a couple of feet to reach the surface of the floor.

At the end of the dim corridor were stairs and when he reached the base he looked up and saw her standing on the top step. She was smiling down at him with eyes as bright as a schoolgirl's, and when he had neared the top she came down the last two steps to meet him.

They stared at each other for a moment, then averted

their eyes. She picked up one of his hands, carried it to her face and kissed it. Then she abruptly turned away to lead him into a big room just off the landing.

This was obviously her home, though it was barely fit for habitation. The floor was tilted and seemed to bounce as he walked across it. An old mattress lay in a corner under the only section of wall that had not been water damaged. A crude table stood next to one of the open windows and a small trunk sat at the foot of the mattress. Except for a meager store of supplies on the tabletop and a single flower in a glass tumbler on the windowsill there was nothing else in the room.

Uncorking a bottle she began to pour the last of its wine into the only glasses she possessed. Ledyard watched as she tried to level the glasses, pouring one into the other in front of her eyes. He thought she must be terribly brave to be hanging on like this.

He stepped into her back, placing each of his hands tenderly on her hips. The French woman stiffened and took his hands in hers, running them slowly up her sides and letting them come to rest on her chest. Then she placed her hands over his and began to knead her breasts.

Ledyard buried his nose in her hair and pushed his lips through to her neck. He was already hard against her bottom and she was moving into him with greater and greater pressure.

She turned her face to him and they kissed. She looked so sad and so beautiful . . . it made him crazy. Gripping the wooden sides of the table she met him with all her strength. They combined instantaneously, each body driving itself against the other as if in death throes.

When they were finished she slid off the table and

busied herself by performing a quick inventory of her stores. While she studied the items on the crude table she told Ledyard with gestures that she was going out to find something to eat.

Completing her calculations she tied a kerchief around her neck, led him to the outside and disappeared into a clump of foliage. He was about to follow her when she burst back through the green pushing a bicycle.

Ledyard's head filled with a million thoughts as he watched her pedal past the holes in the drive until she turned and vanished.

There was nothing ill he could think of her, and he felt lucky beyond his dreams because what was happening was real. She was more than the most perfect person he could ever have imagined himself with; she was an agent of monumental change.

Until now he had not been aware of what a ravishing thing life could be. The incredible emotion that was running between them was like a two-way stream of electricity and he recognized it as the most powerful, life affirming force he had ever encountered. The excitement of their union had bestowed in him the conviction that he must always live life this way . . . to the fullest.

Undoubtedly, Ledyard was experiencing some of the normal sensations of romantic love, elevation and certain bravura, but at the same time a unique and agreeable peace had settled into him. So much seemed clear now. No dilemma seemed insurmountable. Death was of no particular consequence.

He had wanted to serve beauty as he lived in the moment, and in the space of a few hours his most ardent dream had been realized.

Ledyard was going down to check on Drayton when he saw the long ladder reaching to the roof and was struck by an impulsive desire to know where he was. Fetching the binoculars from the barn he dashed back and climbed the ladder. If he was quick enough he might still be able to catch a glimpse of her.

He scrambled over the tiles toward the front of the house and found a good observation post on the edge of the destruction. Scanning the road that led from the drive he swept past a line of open fields until a tree-shrouded town sprang into view. There, riding at the bottom of the image was his lover, pedaling up the grade leading into the isolated hamlet.

The town looked like it had been ravaged regularly over a long period. Half of the buildings had been destroyed, and those still intact carried wounds from fire and explosion. He could see a few souls scattered about the fringes of the ancient settlement, all of them with heads bent in the attitude of scavengers. A group of ragged men stood in the middle of the road butchering a horse.

He was uneasy about her going into such a forlorn place and watched until she vanished again. Then he swung the binoculars around to the sound of artillery, coming from what he thought was the south.

There was a long line of smoke at the furthest edge of his vision. In the foreground he could see a tide of activity – trucks and animals and men, criss-crossing the various roads with the uncanny energy of ants. They had to be a part of the front, and it was disconcerting to be unable to identify them as friend or foe. He guessed it was the enemy.

Ledyard made a slow descent on the creaky ladder and went back to the house. He needed a bracer and wanted his portion of the wine.

Sitting on the ledge of the window, he sipped prudently from his glass and began to think about how remarkable it was to have done what they had done without sharing more than a few words.

Shifting on the sill, he looked around the room, wondering if there was anything inside the four walls that could tell him more about her.

His eyes naturally fell on the small trunk at the front of the mattress.

The clasp was unlocked. Ledyard knelt in front of it and guiltily lifted the lid. A layer of clothes, consisting of a moth-eaten sweater, two threadbare dresses and a pair of socks, lay folded across the top. He lifted the sweater to his nose and savored the smell of her before taking the garments out and placing them to one side.

The rest of the space was occupied by seven framed photographs, each one wrapped individually in butcher paper. Two of the pictures were of children, both boys, a couple of years apart. The oldest might have been ten.

The largest photo was of a young sculptor. He stood in front of a block of stone, hammer and chisel poised for action, a look of resolve etched on his handsome face. The remaining images were of two elderly couples, a middle-aged couple, and a group of three teenaged girls, one of whom looked like his lover.

There was no way of determining who the people were or what their relation might be, but it was clear that the likenesses were important. Their individual wraps and pristine conditions stood out like treasure in the pitiful room of the devastated house.

A little wave of sadness passed through Ledyard as he

examined the portraits. All of the people looked normal, even happy. He wondered what might have happened to them since the onset of war. Surely they could not be the same now. They might even be dead.

It was late afternoon before a solitary cyclist came into view and pedaled down the drive toward Ledyard. He had been pacing around the ruined fountain for more than an hour, beseeching God to send her back to him.

She had not been gone long before all of Ledyard's energy focused on her coming back, but as hours passed his fear and frustration raced toward hysteria. He only checked on Drayton once, and when he did it was not with the same urgency. The affection was still there, but for now Drayton was second in the field of love.

At last Ledyard was able to wave his arms and hop into the air. When she was nearer he could see that she was riding with only one hand. The other was steadying a crate balanced on the handlebars.

He caught her as she rolled to a stop. "I'm glad to see you," he said, laughing anxiously, "Oh, am I glad to see you."

She dropped the bicycle, took the crate out of his hands, set it quickly and carefully on the ground and threw her arms around his neck, pressing her open mouth against his. Breathless, she broke away to sequester the bicycle.

On her return she squatted happily in front of the crate and shared with him the fruits of her long shopping. She held up the contents of the crate, identifying the items in turn. Matches, wine, half a loaf of stale bread and some candle scraps were displayed in a perfunctory way. She was proud of two tins of sardines and equally haughty over a small pack of crackers and a one-ounce jar of preserves.

With an ecstatic flourish she held aloft a puny, bruised orange.

The last object in the crate she rose up solemnly. It was wrapped in a torn piece of fabric. She turned one of Ledyard's hands palm up and placed it there, encouraging him to unwrap it himself.

He glanced at her as he pulled at the edge of the dirty cloth. Inside was a clump of tobacco and a few rolling papers.

"You didn't even know I smoked," he laughed and took her into his arms.

They made love on the mattress almost as soon as they arrived back in her room. It was fast but gratifying, and afterwards Ledyard sat naked on the edge of the bed, rolling a cigarette while she made up their modest feast.

Conservation was uppermost in their minds and, despite being hungry, neither one ate much – half of the bread, a cracker each, one tin of sardines and a few sips of wine. They spoke little as they ate, but they were thinking the same thing. Both wanted to save most of what they had for the night.

When they were finished, the lovers walked down the path and into the fields to find Drayton. He had wandered far in his foraging and for a moment he watched the approach of the two people with suspicion. Recognizing Ledyard he squealed rather than whinnied and started immediately to meet him.

His wound had healed and, if it had ever bothered him, Drayton seemed totally unaware of it now. He seemed to have gained a few pounds, and Ledyard was delighted to see him looking so fit.

Ledyard had brought the bridle along to take him

back and jumped on top of him. He extended a hand to the French woman and she swung up behind him.

Drayton danced in place under them, nodding his head impatiently, and Ledyard let him move out at a controlled canter. They rolled ahead through the wheat as if they were riding a rocking chair, and when they reached a level place with good visibility, Ledyard pulled her hands tighter around his waist and let Drayton go.

Drayton reached full speed in seconds. He was fast and straight and there seemed no limit to his power. The lovers sat as easily on the rocketing horse as if he were a magic carpet. Ledyard guided him up a gentle slope, bringing him to a halt on the brow of a low hill.

"Oh my God," she exclaimed, "he is wonderful . . . magnificent!"

Drayton was too charged to stand still and Ledyard let him ease into another canter that carried them along the backbone of the hill. At the end of the ridge was a drop off, and when they jogged over the edge a convoy of several enemy trucks parked along a back road loomed into view less than a hundred yards in front of them.

Milling about the trucks and sprawled in the grass at the side of the road were soldiers. All eyes seemed to be staring curiously at the oncoming horse and riders.

Knowing that it was too late to turn back Ledyard concentrated on masking his shock. He didn't stop but trotted resolutely on. When they were within fifty yards of the trucks, he changed direction and eased Drayton into a leisurely lope.

Now they were traveling parallel to the enemy. He could see many worn faces staring back at him. They were like lions, watching their prey with quiet, emotionless eyes.

Ledyard lifted a hand and smiled.

"Wave," he whispered through his teeth and the French woman moved a hand back and forth in the air. A few soldiers returned the gesture listlessly, but the majority did nothing but continue to stare.

The lovers rode away without being pursued and made straight for home. It had been a sobering encounter, and they walked back to the barn in telling silence. The monstrous war was near, its misery prowling the boundaries of the careless passion that had renewed them.

In the twilight Drayton drank three basins of water then turned and walked into the barn, leaving Ledyard and the French woman to ascend the path alone.

Exhausted, they climbed onto the little mattress and lying back to back, fell asleep.

It was nearly dark when Ledyard woke. He could see her in silhouette, sitting at the open window. A second later her head turned and she stepped to the crude table.

Picking up a box of matches she had brought from the town, the French woman struck one and lit the three leftover candles. Then she returned to the window.

Ledyard joined her and they sat together saying nothing as the light outside wasted away. Their brush with the war had muted what little desire they had for speech, and when they finally turned their faces on one another the silence remained.

There was enough light from the candles to see her eyes and to Ledyard they looked more sad and hopeless than ever. His eyes roamed her face and found nothing that he did not love.

With a finger he traced her sensuous mouth, taking his time. She parted her lips, just enough to let him feel the wetness inside. He leaned forward slowly and kissed her.

Their lovemaking had so far been urgent but now it was unhurried. They knew that they could have anything they wanted, and what they wanted most was for every moment to last as long as possible.

Afterward they lay panting, perfectly content in the gloom of the old, broken house. Their needs had been met, and it didn't matter whether the world outside was engulfed in terror.

Ledyard rolled a cigarette while she fetched the nearly full wine bottle and the two glasses. They sat in peaceful silence, smoking and drinking and watching the play of candlelight.

He wondered now, as he had so often, about the strangeness of being wildly intimate without the benefit of speech.

There was nothing wrong about it, and he speculated that it must be heightening the magnetism between them. He had nothing with which to compare, but when he passed the cigarette, he smiled at her and thought, "It could never be more powerful than this."

Still, he ached to express himself vocally, a desire that led him quite unexpectedly to hum. It was a lament called "The Streets of Laredo," and Ledyard was soon singing of a young, dead cowboy in a low, sweet voice. Catching the tune, the French woman began to hum with him and they sat in the candlelight, harmonizing together, until the song was finished.

They devoured the last of the food and stretched out together on the bed for a smoke. Their minds were busy as they shared the cigarette. Each one was going over the unforgettable scenes of their history, an activity that led to an inevitable return of longing.

Earlier, in the midst of one of their couplings, Ledyard had wondered how long his body could hold out and if he would be able to make it work if she wanted him again. The fears were so far unfounded. He had gotten excited every time.

It was as if the physical part of him lived separate from the mental. Sometimes it was as though he was watching himself from a distance. But on each of their comings together the physical and mental connection made him feel like an individual force on earth. It was the most irresistible feeling he had ever known.

As they lay smoking in the dark, exhausted by love, they knew that as long as they were side by side they would make love again. They would keep making love until they burned themselves up.

They had made love past midnight and when sleep finally overtook them it came with a heaviness that kept them from dreaming or waking till the morning. It was the longest, most satisfying night they would ever have.

VISITORS

Ledyard woke the next morning feeling restless. He lay blinking at the peeling paint on the ceiling trying to pinpoint the source of his anxiety. The thought that he might be getting tired of her passed through him but when he turned and saw her sleeping so innocently he could not picture being without her.

Perhaps it was the future that had put him on edge. The future had been held off, but eventually it would assert itself. A course of action would have to be taken, but what form it might assume eluded him. It was maddening to contemplate the unsolvable, and desperate for movement, he pulled on his pants and shirt and went down to turn Drayton out.

Along the path his anxiety grew, and when he saw Drayton standing alone just outside the barn, a profound sense of emptiness enveloped him. Drayton was alone. They were all alone. There was no form to their lives, no foundation from which to build.

But what could he do? He was thousands of miles from the only home he knew, passing his days in a ruined house with a woman he loved but did not know, with a horse to whom he was desperately devoted but would not be able to protect if the war descended on them again. "If," he thought, "there is no if about it. The war will find us all."

He spent a few minutes with his friend, touching him and telling him how much he cared and how sorry he was to have left him alone lately.

"We'll figure something out," he said aloud. "I won't leave you, Drayton. I promise."

What might happen from here on out was no clearer as Ledyard went back up the path. But he felt a new pressure, the crush of something unknown that had to be faced. He did not know where it was coming from or what to do about it. But its weight was getting heavier.

She was staring at him as he came around the front of the house. Her face looked ready to crack as she stood still and straight next to the fountain. The woman took a few steps and hugged him. There was no hunger in her embrace, only desperation.

"I was afraid," she gasped, "I thought you had left me. I didn't know what to do."

As he listened to her, Ledyard heard another sound and they both turned to see a man on a bicycle pedaling toward them.

Ledyard's first instinct was to run, but he had already been seen. Besides, the man on the bicycle was a civilian, and he decided it might be better to hear what their visitor had to say.

The man slowed to a stop, threw a leg over the seat and walked his bicycle the few remaining feet to where they were standing.

His clothes were rumpled and dirty, and heavy stubble was erupting on his face. A mustache dropped from his upper lip adding to his downtrodden look. Dirt looked as if it had been poured into the lines of his face. The sole of one of his shoes had separated from the toe.

But his eyes were warm and possessed the helpless air of a man whose best years had passed. Ledyard guessed him to be about sixty.

"Good morning," he said to the French woman, "did you like the wine?"

"Yes, it was delicious."

"That's good." He nodded toward Ledyard.

"I don't believe I know this gentleman."

She glanced furtively at Ledyard. She had no idea what to say to the man with the bicycle.

Looking at her lover she said some words about the man with the bicycle Ledyard did not understand. Ledyard knew the man was asking about him and innocently stuck out his hand.

"I'm Ledyard."

"Ledyard," the visitor repeated. He took a long look at the soldier in ill-fitting civilian clothes and to Ledyard's shock, said in precise English: "Are you British?"

Ledyard looked at him with such concentration that for a moment the stranger thought he might be attacked.

"I'm an American."

"American?" The visitor seemed puzzled. "What are you doing here?"

"I'm lost," Ledyard said flatly.

The visitor scratched the side of his head. He seemed exasperated. In a quick, casual manner he glanced at the lovers with traces of concern. "I am Gerard . . . but I am called Sasha by everyone." he said with a smile.

"We must have a talk."

"A talk?" Ledyard replied blankly, "About what?"

"About her."

"I have nothing to tell you about her."

"But I have something to tell you."

Ledyard stared back at him. "I'm not sure I want to hear what you have to say."

"I was just introduced to you as a man she did business with yesterday, that I was someone she had met for the first time. But that is not true. I have known her since the day she was born." Before Ledyard could reply Sasha turned to the French woman and informed her that he was affiliated with underground forces and that it was imperative that he have an immediate informational chat with the American. For security reasons, no one could monitor their conversation.

The French woman stood still, blinking at him. Sasha was more than affiliated with the underground. He was one of the few remaining originals in the region, the war having taken most of them.

Sasha suspected Ledyard had nothing of practical value to tell, but as Ledyard soon discovered, there was much that Sasha had to impart.

In tense silence, the two men followed the path to the barn. Drayton was inside, and watched curiously as Ledyard and the stranger sat down in the hay.

Sasha was uneasy. "This woman," he began but stopped. Ledyard had noticed that his warm eyes had grown much keener as the wheels of thought turned in his head. "How long have you been here?"

"I'm not sure," Ledyard answered, "two days . . . three."

"The woman you are with, what do you know about

her?"

"Nothing?"

"Her name?"

"No."

"I know her name," Sasha said, "Her name is Nicole Denbo. She's not in her right mind." Ledyard blinked but said nothing. "Do you know she was married?" Sasha asked.

"No, I didn't but . . ."

"Well, I know because she was married to my son. He was shot on suspicion of being in the resistance . . . over a year ago. He wasn't in the resistance. He was a sweet, artistic boy."

"I'm sorry," Ledyard whispered.

"They had two sons. Shelling killed them both . . . up in the house. Nicole's parents were both killed and her two sisters and her brother. I am the only member of her family who is not dead, but I have not been enough for her. Others and myself have tried to make her leave that house of ghosts, but she has always refused. And now she does not know who she is. You are dealing with a woman who has lost everything but her grief."

"What am I supposed to do?"

"I will do my best to get you back through the lines."

"I can't leave her," Ledyard said lowly. Sasha brushed this aside.

"You have to."

"I can't."

"You love her?" Sasha asked.

"Yes."

"You have to pardon me now, but I have to say you don't know what you are doing." Ledyard said nothing.

Sasha thought.

"Alright," he said finally, "we'll see what we can do with a man and a woman. But I warn you . . . she may not go with you."

"I think she will," Ledyard answered stoically. Sasha looked at Drayton as he had occasionally during their talk. "If you don't mind I would like to take the horse. Meat is very scarce."

"The horse goes too."

Sasha looked at Ledyard as if he were crazy. "The war has made everyone insane," he said lamentably, staring down at the hay with a shake or two of his head. He pulled a notebook from his jacket and tore out a page.

"The best I can do for you will be to make a map of the area. The English are close in the south, but it would take a miracle of the highest order to reach them.

Ledyard looked down at his lap, considering what Sasha had said. Whatever action they took would be independent of any real help. Doomed as he felt, Ledyard could not think of abandoning either Drayton or the French woman.

"I could use a map."

Sasha charted out the area noting towns, troop concentrations, major roads, woods and streams. When he was finished he offered bits and pieces of advice as to which routes might hold the best chances of success.

As they followed the path back to the house, a human voice brought them to a sudden halt. The voice was distant but somehow near, and the few words they had heard were enough to tell them that the speaker was German.

They jumped off the path and stealthily made their way through the trees, heading toward the house.

There was nothing the French woman could have done. The arrival of Sasha had punched a hole in the false wall she had constructed, allowing a few memories to leak back into her head. Agitated, she had taken his bicycle for a ride and was halfway down the drive when the small convoy suddenly turned off the road and came toward her.

She pedaled back and waited at the fountain as the vehicles came to a halt. A young officer stepped out of a car as a dozen soldiers clambered out of the truck behind him.

He spoke enough French to make himself understood and told her that he was going to look the house over as a possible headquarters. The French woman said that the place was all she had, and that it was ruined.

She was two people as she spoke. One was standing in the driveway, talking calmly to a German officer. The other was a receptacle of remembrance. She saw her husband clearly. He was kissing her. The two boys were at play, racing through the house. She was happy and alive and complete.

But that was no more.

When she saw Sasha coming around the corner she suddenly remembered Ledyard and knew in an instant that no matter how hard she might try, the pieces of herself would never be put together again. Her life was finished . . . for the second time.

There was only one thing to do and, as Sasha approached the officer, saying something about the condition of her mind, she focused on the revolver the German wore about his waist, particularly the undone flap of the holster.

Knowing he might have to withdraw at any moment, Ledyard stayed in a crouch, watching the scene through an opening in a pile of rubble. For a few moments everything seemed ordinary, three people having a discussion. But without the slightest warning the scene shifted to a macabre spectacle of chaos and death.

Ledyard looked on stupefied as the French woman suddenly plucked the officer's gun from its holster. Covering his head, the German fell to the ground expecting to be shot as the troops behind reflexively raised their weapons.

The French woman pointed the barrel of the pistol at her own chest and fired twice. At the same time the German soldiers discharged their rifles and several more bullets slammed into her. Some of the soldiers fired over their prone officer and hit Sasha who collapsed immediately.

The officer got to his feet while a cloud of gun smoke was still lifting and went from one body to another. At each he glanced back at his men for enlightenment, but they had none to give. It had happened too fast.

Ledyard saw none of this. He was already streaking back to the barn. Crossing the yard, he scooped up the French helmet standing next to the pump and dashed into the barn. He had to have the binoculars. They were somewhere in the hay and he searched feverishly until at last he had them.

Just as he leaped onto Drayton's back the barn door swung open.

Four enemy soldiers stood silhouetted in bright daylight. They heard a sound but never saw Ledyard and Drayton coming. The soldiers went down like ten pins under the sudden onslaught of horse and rider and by the time they picked themselves out of the dirt and readied their weapons, the runaways had disappeared.

RIDING SOUTH

Ledyard galloped into the south with a devastated heart. He was all heart now, a thing of pure feeling, a glass vessel struck by a hammer.

Everything that had happened was unthinkable, and he was no longer sure how to behave. He had lost his equilibrium in a headlong fall, a tumbling free form dive into nightmare. He knew that he must ride away from it but he did not know how to do it.

Fortunately, Drayton did. The horse was glad to be in the open again, carrying weight. Not that he liked carrying weight, but Drayton had learned that the burden on his back somehow represented freedom and when they had raced clear of the barn he settled into a steady canter.

The rider on his back seemed heavier today and not as crisp, and Drayton felt a lack of connection. This proved out when he tired, dropping first into a trot, then a walk without feeling any kind of signal from above.

What Drayton felt but did not know was that it took Ledyard's mind half an hour to rebuild enough cohesion to make thought possible. When he was finally able to take stock of himself, he realized that they were as alone and vulnerable as they had ever been. All he possessed was a shirt, a pair of pants, the French helmet and the binoculars. He had no weapon, and his feet were bare.

They continued in a southerly direction until they reached the vaguely familiar hill country of the long, untended vineyard and found the same cistern that had been the site of their meeting with the German.

The water was as cool and clear as it had been before, and when they had drunk their fill Ledyard lay down and gazed up at the cloud-filled sky.

The clouds were in the swift currents of air high above, and as he watched them speed by he was reassured. No matter what happened in human events, he told himself, the great earth would keep on turning just as it was now. Human endeavor, whether in love or work or war, was nothing compared with the action of the seas, the massive swirling of the skies or the incessant spinning of the mighty sphere on which he now lay.

There was nothing he could do but sleep, so he closed his eyes and passed the rest of the afternoon and night with barely a stir.

When he woke shortly after dawn, the first thing he saw was Drayton's face hovering over his. There was a simple purity in the horse's countenance that reassured him in the same way the drifting clouds had quieted his trauma the afternoon before.

Ledyard sat up with sudden clarity. The only way to get away from the war was to return to it. Clandestine attempts to procure food or escape the enemy no longer seemed important. He would ignore his hunger and the enemy.

Staying alive seemed less important too. Action was

what Ledyard wanted. The reaching of a single goal was now his guide, his salvation, his reason for being and if he and Drayton died together that would be fine.

When he studied the map Sasha had given him he understood exactly what should be done. Two towns were marked on the paper, then a wood, then the front. He would pass through the towns, picking up anything he might be able to use, traverse the wood and emerge at the front. Then he would study the lines and take his best chance.

Only death could stop him and, feeling a driving need to reach his goal, he jumped on Drayton's back and they set off, angling east to pick up the road that led to the first of the two towns.

Buried in his mind was the logical knowledge that said the closer he got to the fighting the more crowded the road would become. He had not yet admitted this to himself, preferring to indulge the fantasy of some secret corridor he might sneak through.

But the road told a different story.

It was well traveled, in fact choked with a seething mixture of soldiers and civilians. Lines of the weary and war torn passed back and forth. They were harassed by trucks and motorcycles, horses and wagons and miserable handcarts, all inching toward some destination, imploring the people on foot to give way.

Ledyard despised it all: the destruction, the war, the waste, the insanity. He despised the people on the road. The war could stop, but it wouldn't because they didn't rise against it.

For the moment he had blotted out the French woman. She was active in his memory, but he had succeeded in relegating her status to that of a war victim, one of millions of sad, horrifying stories.

He hated the war with a new depth that produced cunning. As he passed the binoculars back and forth along the road he noticed several wounded civilians wobbling to their destinations. They gave him an idea.

With his teeth he ripped one of the arms off his white shirt and tore it into strips. He slipped out of the shirt and pants and used them to rub Drayton, transferring much of the sweat and dirt on the horse's coat to the garments.

Spitting into the clothes until his mouth was dry, he put them back on and rolled in the dirt.

He found a slim, tough twig, sharpened it with a rock and used it as a scalpel, opening an inch-long line in his forehead. The blood pumped furiously from his head, and as it did he wrapped it with the strips he had made. When they were soaked in his own blood he rolled his head in the dirt.

When he had stopped bleeding, he jumped up on Drayton and they rode toward the road, there to take their places as anonymous victims of war riding toward the front.

The bandage around his head provided the added advantage of obscuring much of his face and no one gave him more than cursory attention when he and Drayton walked out of a field and took a place among those headed south.

It was much easier than he had expected.

Like everyone else, they moved like sleepwalkers. Ledyard kept his head low and his expression blank. People spoke to him, including one German soldier but no one bothered him further when he feigned shock by not replying.

The only tension came with a sudden stampede to a Red Cross truck that was distributing flying bread to an ocean of outstretched arms. Ledyard was pushing closer to the front of the crowd when a small loaf caromed off a man's head, bounced against Ledyard's chest and ended up in one of his hands.

Holding his prize high he turned and rode out of the throng. He planned to parcel out the bread in small pieces, masticate it into liquid and, in so doing, create an impression of having eaten more than was really there. But the loaf was long gone before he reached the first of the two towns on Sasha's map.

It was a patchwork of caved-in buildings, chewed up streets and tattered residents. The enemy moved freely among the remains of the populace but Ledyard had grown so astute in his role as a war victim that he no longer feared them and passed through the hamlet without being questioned.

Just beyond the village was a small stream, from which people were carrying water and doing laundry. As he paused to take in a few mouthfuls of dirty water he noticed that a man dangling a line in the water had a sudden strike. He watched as the angler jerked at the line and a rotting boot flew out of the water. The fisherman undid the hook, turned the shoe in his hand and, to Ledyard's surprise, slipped it into a gunnysack. "Only in war," Ledyard thought, "could a man land trash and think of it as a catch."

There was a sordidness in the desperation around them and as they continued down the road to the last town, Ledyard felt strangely queasy.

The traffic had dropped considerably, and every grim face he passed looked at him with despair. More precisely, they looked at Drayton, and Ledyard soon realized that the spark of life he saw when their eyes fell his way was envy for the meat moving under him.

As time passed, the penetrating gaze of his fellow wanderers became unbearable and Ledyard gradually lowered his chin to his chest. He could not stop traveling, but he did not have to look at them.

At twilight the town closest to the front came into view. From afar he had seen the spidery remains of a steeple, and as he entered the town he found that the church was the only edifice in a state that could remotely be considered as standing.

The spire itself was a freak of physics, a tottering assemblage of bricks and mortar that wound toward the sky like a tower of playing cards. The church proper was like everything else in the town, a wrecked shell of its former splendor. A few pieces of roof ribbing were suspended in space while below a hodge-podge of broken pews and plaster and other pieces of the building lay together as if they had been shaken and poured. Part of a rear wall remained, and he could see the remnants of the savior on the cross. All that remained of him was a pectoral, a shoulder and a bicep.

Jesus, too, had been blown away, like everything else in the path of war.

There weren't many people about, mostly women and children and those that seemed haunted. Scrawny widows accompanied by ragged broods interrupted their scavenging to follow him with hollow eyes. Men, grouped in twos and threes as they idled on what had once been corners, followed him with the same unblinking gazes, and Ledyard was relieved to reach the far boundary of the town.

The sound of artillery had been increasing steadily, and as they started onto the open road the boom of it was even more distinct, leading him to believe the front could be no more than a mile or two away.

He had been scouting the wooded ridges bordering either side of the highway, and when he turned his attention back to the road he pulled Drayton up short. All traffic had evaporated, and directly ahead enemy troops were standing around, flanked by a collection of vehicles. It was a checkpoint.

Turning Drayton about, Ledyard started back to the desolate town. Glancing over his shoulder he tried to make a mental map of the approach to the most heavily wooded ridge. He would come back as night deepened, sleep in the cover of the trees, and make his way to the front early in the morning. In the meantime he would investigate the annihilated town. He was certain the people had nothing to give, but he might get lucky and stumble across a few scraps of food or at least some water.

There was firelight ahead, and soon he could make out knots of civilians gathered around blazes they had made in discarded barrels. It was strange to see people out at night, conducting personal business in the open, and yet there was a queer, routine quality to the gatherings, as if the participants were performing a desultory ritual.

The lively lights of flames only made the solemn faces he had seen earlier more woebegone, and as Ledyard rode past, a sense of foreboding tingled in his scalp. The people did not talk or smile or acknowledge him in any way save with their cryptic gazes. They seemed not to move, and as Ledyard and Drayton rode deeper into what had once been a settlement of homes and shops and public buildings, the idea came to him that the people who now existed there were really dead. Their hearts still beat, but the light was gone from their eyes.

He could hear an odd scuttling out in the dark, the same sound that scurrying rodents make in the night. But this was a larger sound and he knew that there were people scrambling past him. Though he had been given no reason to fear them, he was certain that their dark movements were directed at him.

A flame flickered and came alive in the blackness at the end of the road, and as he watched, it moved from side to side. More lights flared. Then they began to move.

Ledyard and Drayton stood alone in the mangled road, watching as the flames, which he now realized were torches, marched steadily toward them.

He glanced back over his shoulder. A similar configuration of light was advancing on him from behind. He thought briefly that he might have blundered into some kind of ceremony and wanted to move out of the way. But the vague, mountainous outlines of war refuse walled him in on both sides.

Gradually, he could see shadows of the torch-bearing villagers, and as the distance between them shrank, Ledyard could no longer disregard the malice descending about him.

Drayton felt it too. He had begun to shift uneasily from one foot to another.

The torch lines came to a shuffling halt a few yards on either side of him, and a voice called out from the darkness.

Ledyard did not understand the words, and after a moment of silence the voice repeated the words again.

It was a command.

The torch carriers started forward warily. There was a sullen cast to every face and all at once Ledyard knew what they desired. They wanted Drayton.

The horse reared up as the first hand clutched at Ledyard's leg, trying to pull him to ground. Drayton wheeled through the air and Ledyard drove the binoculars down on someone's skull. The crowd fell back momentarily and hugging his neck Ledyard turned Drayton into the group that had come up from behind.

As their hands clawed at his bridle the horse rose into the air once more bringing his sharp hooves down on the head of a woman. As she fell back screaming Drayton gave a mighty kick with both hind legs and more screams crashed against the wild shouts that were swirling around them.

Swinging the binoculars like a mace, Ledyard concentrated on the mass he now faced. Drayton was rearing continually and between the two of them they began to clear a path. The desperate villagers melted away and suddenly horse and rider were free.

As they broke clear, a thrown brick caught Ledyard between the shoulder blades. Reeling against the blow, he listed crazily on Drayton's back. But holding on by a heel, he managed to right himself, and they clattered back up the street at a gallop.

When they had cleared the town, he looked back. Torchlight was still dancing in the night, but it was not following him. Slowing Drayton to a trot, they veered left off the road, and soon the ground was rising toward the trees he knew were waiting for him on top of the ridge.

It was a moonless night, and he could see nothing as they made their way slowly up. When they reached the trees Ledyard dismounted and they walked through the woods on foot. Every few minutes he would drop down and run his hands over the ground to see how tall the grass was. When he was finally satisfied, he pulled off Drayton's bridle and stretched out on the bare ground.

THE LUCK OF THE WIND

Ledyard spent a fitful night on the ground atop the ridge. The thump-like bang of artillery made it impossible to sleep, and the best he could do was drift on and off, willing himself into the twilight state that precedes unconsciousness.

The void of his wakefulness admitted uncounted thoughts.

He was tormented by involuntary images of the French woman, but was too fearful of the pain that might come if he let himself think of her.

He wondered anxiously if a retreating enemy might overrun him. Anything could happen this near to the fighting, and he could expect no warning. He cringed at the thought of a fleeing soldier pausing in flight to shoot him, and could not think of what might happen to Drayton.

Every random sound in the woods made him wonder if the hungry villagers might be upon them again.

He could not remember how many days he had been wandering, nor could he begin to recount all that had happened but he knew he must be close to the front . . . at the end of his long run.

Tomorrow would likely be the last day he would ever see. As the artillery crescendoed, it was difficult for him to tell if he had really fallen asleep and was dreaming or if he was speculating through a fog of fatigue. He saw himself and Drayton tumbling through the air in pieces, body parts blown to bloody pulp. He imagined the two of them whole, standing on the broad deck of a ship sailing to New York City. He fantasized about a dwelling, part stall, part home, which both of them shared. He saw them flying over the German lines.

The acrid odor of bomb smoke was in his nose all night and at first light he realized that the mist curling through the trees was actually the residue of explosions.

Not knowing what else to do, they moved forward, and a hundred yards later Ledyard stopped to listen. There were noises ahead, sounds of work mixed with human voices.

Jumping down, Ledyard tied Drayton's reins to a low limb and crept ahead. The trees thinned out quickly and in moments gave way to a wide clearing beyond which was limitless sky.

A dozen enemy soldiers occupied the open space, an observation unit Ledyard suspected. Most of them were hurrying about, packing gear while two officers stood on what appeared to be the edge of a cliff, staring at the sky through binoculars as they chatted back and forth.

The small cadre of men began to move out, and Ledyard blinked uncomprehendingly as they disappeared before his eyes. The departing soldiers seemed to walk off into the sky, each one gradually vanishing below the horizon.

When the last head had sunk from sight and the

clearing was still, Ledyard backtracked and brought Drayton up. Advancing into the clearing, he quickly discovered the solution to the mystery of the disappearing soldiers.

The open space was the lip of a natural bench perched at the edge of a great promontory that jutted over a long plain. When Ledyard looked down it seemed that the entire world was spreading before him.

The face of the promontory fell away in a long gentle slope of a thousand feet and Ledyard saw that the observation party had reached the bottom. They were headed for a busy staging area behind the lines. Though partially obscured by smoke, he could see vehicles and horses and tents. Scores of soldiers were scurrying about their business with an urgency that gave Ledyard the impression that they might be preparing for an assault.

He lifted the binoculars to examine what he could of the smoke-shrouded plain beyond and saw that allied artillery was still landing. If an attack were to come it seemed likely that it would be the allies who would go over the top, as they always did after one of their own barrages.

The morning's breeze was growing at his back and soon his shirt was rippling in a wind that raced past him and down onto the plain, effectively sweeping away low-lying clouds of smoke and providing him with a clear view of the entire battlefield.

In front of the staging area was the first of four trenches, each spaced about one hundred yards apart. They faced south, like a line of ocean swells. Beyond the dust of these man-made cuts lay the familiar open swath of no-man's land.

Squinting through the glasses, he could make out

the fortifications of the allies far in the distance. A flag was flying from the first of the entrenchments. Ledyard lowered the glasses, rubbed his eyes, lifted the binoculars once more and was able to see the distinctive pattern of the British Union Jack.

The enemy lines snaked for miles to the right and left but he calculated the distance between himself and the allies as quite short, a mile and a half at most.

The more he surveyed the scene below him however, the more dejected he became. The distance might as well have been a million miles, for there seemed no possible way to traverse it without being killed. The only conceivable way they could cross the enemy positions was through the miracle of flight and he looked briefly at Drayton hoping to see wings growing from his shoulders.

The wind gusted violently as he sat cross-legged on the edge of the promontory, and for want of anything better to do, brought the binoculars back to his eyes and looked out at the battlefield.

All artillery fire had ceased, but something strange was happening at the enemy's forward positions. Men were running onto the battlefield. There was fair distance between them, and though they ran in unison they were not moving in a solid human wave. There seemed no way that so few could be challenging their enemy.

As if on cue, the widely spaced line of soldiers stopped and went to ground in the middle of no-man's land. After minutes, all of them were up and retreating back to the trenches.

Almost immediately gaily colored smoke began to rise from the places where they had paused on the battlefield. At first Ledyard thought they might be signals of some kind, though he could not imagine their purpose.

But as the orange curls billowed, merging into a massive, boiling cloud, he knew that it could only be the thing he had heard so much about but never seen.

Gas.

The great vaporous wall was moving across no-man's land with the speed of an ocean wave, and Ledyard winced at the thought of it washing over the allied lines.

A strange stillness suddenly descended, and with a few, final puffs, the wind blowing at Ledyard's back stopped. It seemed impossible, but when he looked back at the trees on the ridge, which had shortly before been bending to the will of the wind, not a solitary leaf was stirring.

Plucking the binoculars off his lap he sighted toward no-man's land and found that the great, chemical plume had slowed dramatically. Soon the gassy cloud had come to a halt and was beginning to settle toward the ground.

He had heard stories about wind and gas, how the wind had to be just right for a successful attack and that once the gas had settled as far down as a man's waist it was relatively harmless, so long as it wasn't inhaled or taken into the eyes.

Ledyard was too intent on watching to notice the breeze when it returned but as it began to pick up speed he realized that something amazing had happened.

The wind had shifted. It was blowing into his face.

Quickly, he focused on no-man's land and saw that the cloud had already begun to rise. Now it was creeping back the way it had come.

He dropped the glasses down to the furthest German trench, which was now swarming with activity as men scampered down from the ramparts to join those below. All of them were pulling masks over their heads.

The same frantic preparation was being pursued in the remaining three trenches and at the rear staging area. Troops leaped into vehicles and drove off. Horses were being gathered and driven deeper into the rear.

The first wisps of gas had reached the German trenches and, as Ledyard watched, each one was rendered invisible by the suffocating clouds.

The lethal mixture had just begun to envelope the staging area at the base of the promontory when the wind abruptly and mysteriously ceased for the second time, leaving the whole of the enemy lines blanketed in stalled gas.

In a twinkling Ledyard saw his great chance.

He had no idea how long it would take the gas to settle nor did he consider what might happen if the capricious wind rose once more. The only thing he knew for certain was that the multitudes of soldiers in front of him were, for the moment, pinned down. It was the best chance he could ever hope for, and he and Drayton zigzagged down the face of the headland.

The heavy wall of gas had stopped at the edge of the incline and Ledyard watched in awe and frustration as the monster subsided with infuriating slowness.

When it had fallen below Drayton's nostrils they entered at a walk. At once Drayton began to shake his head from side to side. Ledyard's eyes began to burn and he could feel his throat constricting as they passed the murky tents of the enemy. They were both coughing now, their lungs convulsing to repel the noxious traces of poison that had seeped in.

The gas was still belly high when they went over the first trench. The jump was so clean and the silence at their backs so profound that Ledyard felt sure no one had even seen them.

The gas was going to ground quickly and by the time Drayton had sailed over the second and third trenches the carpet of fumes was a foot high.

As they bore down on the last enemy position Ledyard could see a few heads in helmets and masks poking through the orange mist. Drayton gathered himself and just as he soared upward a helmet suddenly rose and collided with one of his hooves.

The stinging impact threw the horse off balance and as he came to earth on the other side Drayton stumbled and skidded along the ground on his knees. Somehow he kept his balance and was up and running before Ledyard could be pitched all the way over his head.

Ledyard aimed for the British flag he had seen and when he was close enough to make out human forms he lifted an arm and began to yell.

"American!" he screamed. "Americaaaan, Americaaaaan!"

The British had seen him coming and the order had gone down the line to hold fire. It was first thought that an enemy soldier was changing sides.

But when word was passed like a fast burning fuse that the oncoming horseman was identifying himself as an American, curiosity drove many to jump onto the fire steps for a better look. If he really was an American emerging from enemy territory through a curtain of gas, it was a sight not to be missed.

Ledyard was yelling all the way and the sight of men

waving back, some with faint shouts of encouragement, made him feel like crying. They had made it. They had triumphed against impossible odds.

And they would have were it not for the over-anxious captain of a mortar crew positioned behind the British lines.

The men had been on duty since the night before and though they were dead on their feet, the captain had insisted that they test fire some recently arrived ordnance.

It had never been thought that anyone would be so foolish as to fire live mortar rounds over the heads of their own troops but the English captain in charge, who had taken command the night before, possessed an ambition that defied logic. He was certain that his initiative would make a deep impression on those above him.

As Ledyard and Drayton streaked across no-man's land, the captain urged his exhausted, bleary-eyed crew to "look sharp" as they made ready to fire, and while he stood around clapping his hands, one of the soon to be court marshaled captain's gunners failed to set his mortar at the proper elevation.

Ledyard was confused when the first shells began to explode behind him. Was the enemy firing at him? Or were the British?

They were still a hundred yards from their goal and he fixed his gaze between Drayton's ears. A small berm crowned with hunks of splintered wood lay dead ahead, flanked by huge craters.

As Ledyard lowered himself on Drayton's neck he heard the incoming whine of a shell. Its whistle was ear splitting and Ledyard actually saw it pass as they lifted into the air. The bomb landed just behind them and its concussive blast skewed their trajectory. Horse and rider separated in space, each body left to fly a course of its own.

Ledyard never saw what happened to Drayton as he spun back to earth, but he saw the stump of the tree. He saw it all the way – even the unique lines of its bark were clear in the moment before it impacted with his head.

REUNION

The dream was the same. They were warm and happy in the void, so content that it was impossible to tell whether they had been voyaging in the blackness of space for five minutes or five years.

The stars beckoned, and before long they were passing over the infinite ribbon of dazzling light. This time, however, they did not dissolve. The stars at their feet grew so bright that they hurt the eyes, and just as the light became unbearable, a voice intruded.

"Open your mouth corporal . . . the spoon is here . . . open your lips."

Ledyard's eyelids lifted, and through a curtain of pain encircling his head he discerned the fuzzy outlines of two men. One sat on the edge of a cot close by, his hands against his ears. An index finger tapped crazily against his temple. Another man crouched at his feet, holding a small bowl in one hand and a spoon in the other. He seemed to be offering food, but the man on the cot would not open his mouth.

Ledyard's eyes were too heavy to keep open, and he lapsed back into sleep.

When he woke again, several men had gathered at the cot next to him. The images were clearer now, but when Ledyard moved his head for a better look, he was seized with a blinding hurt.

When it receded, he looked down and discovered that the man who had been sitting on the cot was now under it. He was curled in a fetal position and his face was grimacing so tightly that it was vibrating. All of him was vibrating.

One of the men around the cot was leaning down, hands on knees.

"There is no bomb Dillingham," he said to the man under the cot. "You are in the hospital. There are no bombs here. You don't hear any bombs, do you? Now come up from there."

Ledyard lay his head back as gently as possible. Even so, a stabbing pain struck in his head. With shut eyes he held his breath until the piercing needles subdued once more.

The next time he woke, two men in British uniforms, a doctor and an orderly, were staring down at him. The doctor's thick mustache moved and Ledyard saw his tongue begin to roll.

"How are you feeling?" Ledyard opened his mouth, unleashing another wave of pain.

"My head hurts."

The doctor nodded solemnly. "You're lucky your skull's not fractured. But you no doubt have a bruise on your brain. And your scalp is severely lacerated."

For the first time, Ledyard realized his head was bandaged. Lifting his right hand, he touched the side of his skull and felt a slick substance against the wraps. The doctor reached out and brought his hand back to his side.

"Reston here is going to change your dressing."

Ledyard blinked by way of reply. The doctor's face seemed suddenly curious.

"Who are you?" he asked. "Everyone wants to know."

"Ledyard Dixon."

"American?"

"Yes."

"Where did you come from?"

Ledyard lay back and blinked into space. "Long story," he said.

"Quite," the doctor replied, leaning a little closer in his eagerness to hear. But Ledyard did not feel like telling stories.

"Where's my horse?"

"Horse?"

"The horse I was riding. Where is he? Is he dead?"

The doctor and orderly glanced at each other. "I don't know," the doctor answered.

Ledyard sat up a few inches and threw one of his legs onto the floor. Before he could make any further move the doctor and orderly were forcing him gently back onto the bed.

"I have to find my horse," Ledyard gasped.

"Yes, yes old boy, I'm sure you do," said the doctor. "But you can't go anywhere at the moment. Reston will inquire after your horse as soon as you have a new bandage. Won't you Reston?"

The orderly only stared at the patient with a faint smile and Ledyard knew there would be no inquiries. But he decided not to make a fuss. He resolved to regain his energy and, as soon as he was able, take matters into his own hands.

For some reason he did not trust these British. He didn't trust anyone.

All his life he had been open to the point of gullibility. But now a seminal change had taken hold. The change was as incontrovertible as the roots of a molar, fixed forever in the bone of his jaw.

The world would always have aspects of beauty, but when it came to human endeavor he might as well be the only person on earth. Whatever feelings of togetherness he had with the human race were gone, and he knew they would never return.

He faced the fact of his aloneness as Reston ministered to his wound and, by the time the orderly had gone, Ledyard had resolved that he would listen to no one but himself. He would rely on his own instincts, the same instincts that had kept him alive to see this day.

Ledyard had never expected to wake up, and the temporary nature of his injury lifted his spirits. His mind seemed to be working, and after a little testing he found that his motor functions were just as intact.

Reassured, he began to plot. It was very possible that Drayton was dead, but if he were alive every minute that passed would make the chances of finding him slimmer. It was imperative that he get out of bed.

He surveyed his surroundings. The wooden building was long and narrow with two lines of cots on either side separated by a wide aisle. There were perhaps fifty beds in total.

After a few minutes observation of his fellow patients, a pattern emerged. All of them seemed disoriented. The man next to him was still shivering on the floor under his cot. Others were moving about but were odd. One man was marching back and forth along the aisle. Another was circling his bed. Another was walking in place at a wall. Another stood, head bowed, mumbling inaudibly to a closed window.

The majority of the patients however, lay rigidly abed, showing no outward sign of injury. It had to be a shell-shock ward, and as Ledyard watched the empty rituals of his companions, he counted himself lucky to have smashed his head against a tree stump.

Carts were pushed into the ward, and food was doled out to the patients. Though pain accompanied each bite and swallow, Ledyard ate a bowl of soup, a hunk of bread and an apple. He needed fuel to make a getaway.

After lunch the doctors made their rounds and Ledyard received another visit from the man with the heavy mustache.

"I can see you're feeling better," he said cheerfully.

"The Americans will be sending someone around in the morning, that's the word I've been given."

"Why?" Ledyard asked flatly.

"Well, they want to see you . . . talk to you . . ." Here the doctor assumed a jaunty air. "Find out what you've been up to I suppose. In the meantime, rest. And sleep as much as you can. I think you'll be fit before you know it." The words "find out what you've been up to" turned over and over in Ledyard's head and no matter how he positioned them they looked suspicious. Perhaps the authorities were skeptical of a single soldier's disappearance and sudden return from enemy country. There would be questions upon questions, removal, reassignment. More questions. Investigations.

Ledyard could afford none of it. If there was any hope

of finding Drayton, the search could not wait another day. The food had made him feel stronger, and after a few minutes of excruciating maneuvers, he managed to gain the edge of the bed and rise to his feet. The first steps were small and shaky, each one releasing a torrent of pain. He had to wait after the landing of each foot for the violent shuddering in his skull to diminish enough to take the next step.

He was worried about his unsteady legs collapsing under him. A fall would be catastrophic. He was still so woozy that he feared he might not be able to get back up.

But Ledyard surmounted these difficulties and before long was walking down the ward's empty aisle. He felt strangely invisible. As he moved from one end of the bay to the other, his fellow patients took no notice of him.

He made two round trips on his first sojourn and by the end of the second was walking with confidence. He reached his bed again moments before the arrival of a pair of orderlies and lay back down with the certainty that he would be up and out as soon as the opportunity presented itself.

While the orderlies performed their duties he noticed that the man next to him, who remained under the cot, had a uniform hanging on the wall behind the bunk. A pair of boots peeked out from the floor at the head of the bed, and Ledyard thought it probable that the whole outfit would fit him.

As soon as the orderlies disappeared he was up and walking. This time he completed several round trips.

By mid-afternoon he was ready. He tried on his neighbor's boots and was delighted at how easily his feet slipped inside.

At four o'clock there was a bevy of activity as tea was served, and when the staff had disappeared, Ledyard swung out of bed and got dressed. The uniform fit, and the boots gave him added stability. He wished himself good luck and walked smartly for the exit.

Pushing through a set of doors Ledyard found himself in a small foyer. In an anteroom several workers were too engaged in a game of cards to notice his passing.

As he slipped through another pair of double doors and stepped onto a short landing, he encountered another orderly who was just ascending a short flight of wooden steps. The orderly hesitated, eyeing him curiously.

"You work here?" Ledyard inquired.

"Yes."

"I'm looking for a man name of Charleton. Edward Charleton."

The orderly thought. "No," he replied.

"Is he shell shocked?"

"I believe so."

The orderly turned and pointed toward a line of buildings across the way.

"Try that one third from the right." Ledyard mumbled a thanks and started down the steps while the orderly disappeared through the doors behind him. Pausing at the foot of the steps, he took in the sprawling encampment. A long, busy avenue ran in front of the hospital barracks. It was crowded with soldiers on foot, in cars and on horseback. Ledyard was reassured to see that men who would be called walking-wounded were common. The turban around his head would not draw more than passing interest.

The American accent was his over-riding concern. He

could not affect an English one, and he made up his mind to muddle his words, speaking coherently but in low, muted tones that would blur the distinctiveness of his tongue. He would also use as few words as possible.

Anxious to put some distance between himself and the ward, he pushed off into the avenue. The encampment went on for as far as he could see and was obviously a hub of operations for the British forces.

He inquired of a man on crutches where he could find the veterinary and was told that it was not far in the same direction he was going.

The horse hospital was a cavernous, hastily constructed barn. Several doctors were at work, and Ledyard loitered next to the first one he saw. The vet, a red-faced man about fifty, was sitting on the neck of a downed horse, working on its face while several soldiers lay piled on the animal, holding him down. The doctor was sewing up a wound on the horse's eye. He tied off the last stitch and, with a word of warning to his assistants, scrambled to one side as the horse leaped to its feet.

The red-faced veterinarian stood still, watching one of the soldiers lead it away.

"Doctor?"

The vet gave Ledyard the once over before he replied, focusing his enigmatic glare on the white turban.

"Yes?"

"I'm looking for a horse."

"What horse?"

"A horse I rode in on yesterday?"

The doctor's glare seemed to darken before his face relaxed. "You're not the American, are you?"

"I suppose I am," Ledyard sighed. Ledyard lied to the

doctor, telling him the horse he sought had been purchased from a Belgian farmer. He gave a detailed description of Drayton but, though he thought hard about it, the doctor could not recall seeing an animal of that description.

He told Ledyard that most likely the horse had been killed. The only lead he gave was to check the corrals where used up horses were awaiting shipment to the rendering plants. If the horse he wanted was alive, he might be there.

The holding pens were located at the limits of the military city, and it took half an hour of steady walking to reach them. No sound emanated from more than a hundred horses in the largest enclosure. The animals stood nearly motionless, mute and dejected, all of them suffering from broken spirits.

Ledyard could see that many of them bore terrible wounds. Their despair was so uniform that he felt certain that they knew what was about to happen to them. Not a soul was around to look after them, and Ledyard brazenly called Drayton's name over the sea of condemned animals.

There was no movement in the morose herd, and Ledyard's heart sank with the thought that Drayton was lost to him forever. He stepped onto the middle rail of the fencing, clamped his hands to the sides of his head and called out with all his breath.

"Draytonnnnn!"

At the far end of the packed corral, a head popped out of the misery and Ledyard's call was answered with a squeal of excitement. He rose on the fence and yelled Drayton's name as the horse's form pushed ever closer, moving through the bunched animals as if he was parting the sea.

Impulsively, Ledyard jumped down and pushed

through the mass of listless animals to meet him.

Drayton nickered when Ledyard's arms went around his head but it was half-hearted, and seeing the dull look in his eyes sent a chill through Ledyard.

He looked down Drayton's body and saw a hideous wound. Behind the point of one hip a great chunk of flesh was missing. It was splashed with disinfectant, and some of the coat had been sewn back on in a slip-shod manner. But what had been done was far exceeded by what had not been done.

Most of the flesh in the long, jagged wound was exposed, angry and pink and swarming with insects.

An approaching train whistle jolted Ledyard into action. He led Drayton to the nearest gate and, grabbing a halter hanging on the fence, walked the horse back up the long avenue.

It was a slow trip. Drayton could put almost no weight on the leg connected to the wound, and his gait resembled more a halting hop than a walk. Even in a theatre of war, the wounded man leading a wounded horse rated a second look from everyone they passed, and Ledyard felt relieved when they reached the veterinary barn.

The red-faced doctor was still there. He took one look at Drayton's wound and said, "This horse is finished."

"You mean he won't recover?" Ledyard asked.

"Oh, he'll recover I suppose but . . . he's finished, he's no good to you. He has no value."

"I owe him my own life," Ledyard said, stroking Drayton's muzzle, "many times over."

The plain admission moved something in the red-faced doctor. He stepped closer to the grotesque cavity that represented what was left of Drayton's hip and studied it with his eyes. He pressed his fingertips here and there and commented, "Well, there's not a great deal of structural damage really."

Finally, he stepped back and looked rather sternly at Ledyard. "Your personal property?"

"I have a bill of sale," Ledyard lied.

"Alright . . . my dinnertime is about here. I guess I can do as I please with my own time. Of course I have a fee . . . but . . . ahh . . . I'll waive it if you tell me a few things about the States. Never been over."

For better than an hour the doctor worked on Drayton's decimated side. He asked questions and Ledyard answered. When the doctor announced he had done all that he could and instructed Ledyard on procedures for the dressing he had fashioned, the two men fell into an awkward silence of parting.

Eyeing his handiwork the doctor said to no one in particular, "Quite nice to know that someone wants to save something. Haven't seen that in awhile."

In an off-handed way the doctor offered to let Drayton spend the night at the Crown's expense, and Ledyard accepted.

"But you have to be out at the crack of dawn," the doctor intoned. "That won't be a problem," Ledyard said.

AWAY FROM DANGER

They started up the encampment's main thoroughfare in the darkness of pre-dawn. By first light they had reached a crossroad of the great bivouac, and Ledyard found himself staring at a cluster of homemade arrows tacked on a signpost. Some of the arrows were lettered with the names of nearby towns, but several had a more outlandish cast, indicating the way to places like Paris and Berlin and London.

Ledyard was glad for the whimsical touch, because London was exactly where he wanted to go.

They made steady progress all morning, stopping for water only twice. The second stop was at a pond not far off the road, and when Ledyard looked at the still surface he did not recognize the reflections. He saw a wounded man and a wounded horse, alone in the chaos of a world at war. He laughed at the reflection in the pond for it blasted the limits of credibility. The figures in the pond looked insane, and Ledyard felt in perfect harmony with the madness surrounding them. They were ordinary, typical of the destruction and waste comprising the world, and Ledyard was certain that there was no longer any need to be anxious. No one would stop them; there was no need to do so. Anyone could see that they were already ruined.

Ledyard's prediction was accurate in every detail. When they needed rest, they stopped. When he needed food he simply got in line at a roadside mess. They slept as long as they wanted wherever they could find cover.

In the three days it took them to reach the port of Dunkirk, Ledyard's headaches vanished and Drayton's lameness settled into a routine shuffle.

Ledyard spoke to no one and no one spoke to him. Even to the innately curious, the man and the horse were two pieces of wreckage from which nothing could be gained.

As they came into Dunkirk, a farmer drove a few dairy cows across the road and Ledyard followed him through a gate that opened into a pretty, green pasture. He needed a place to lay up and hoped the farmer might let them sleep in his barn.

The farmer had a daughter who had immigrated to the United States and by virtue of several visits to Pennsylvania had picked up enough English to carry on elementary conversations.

After he heard Ledyard's story, a recounting of his adventures with Drayton which were laid out in a simple, honest way, he warmed to the wounded American and the crippled horse.

The farmer detested the war. A son about Ledyard's age had been lost in the fighting and many of the good memories he had suppressed came back to life in the form of the young man who had wandered onto his property.

He had passively taken every blow of the war for almost four years and found his interest in life rekindled by the opportunity to counter-punch.

The farmer provided them with food and shelter and became an active participant in the execution of Ledyard's plan.

The next morning he drove the American into town and helped him send a telegram to Michigan after which they went to the docks. There the farmer was able to charter a boat at a reasonable price for the short voyage to England.

When a thousand dollars arrived from his father two days later, the first thing Ledyard did was buy several bottles of the best wine he could find. These he presented to his co-conspirator and they sat at the kitchen table late into the night, smoking and laughing.

Early the next morning Drayton walked up the gangplank of the boat they had hired and the two sailed for England.

Within a few hours of their arrival, Ledyard had put Drayton up in the best livery he could find and booked passage for him to New York City.

He took a room for himself in a decent hotel across from the livery and spent the evening composing a second, much longer wire to his father. With great care he laid out in precise detail what he wanted his father to do. He wanted him to meet Drayton's ship and accompany him back to Michigan by train. He stressed the importance of stabling him in a roomy, pleasant place and that whomever he selected for the horse's care had to be reliable. A veterinarian would have to be engaged to monitor the progress of his injury and it was important that his father oversee all of these arrangements. He asked his father to act on faith, because if anything happened to the animal,

Ledyard's own life would lose whatever meaning it retained.

A five-word reply came the next afternoon. "You can rely on me." Ledyard and Drayton parted two days later when he walked his friend into the hold of the ship and settled him into a stall. He pressed money into the hands of every crewman he met and promised the captain a fat bonus if Drayton landed in good health.

Then he stood on the dock, smoking one cigarette after another as the ship sunk below the horizon. Whatever happened now, he knew that Drayton would not be sent down a chute to face the slaughterer's knife.

Though it no longer bothered him from a moral point of view, Ledyard did not have it in him to merely desert.

There was a good chance that no one would ever miss him, but Ledyard could not live life with one eye facing front and one facing behind. Even dying in combat seemed a better alternative, so he opted for a return to the war.

His visit to a private doctor only confirmed what he already knew. The injury to his head was not severe enough to send him home. The concussion was fading and the laceration, while ugly, was in no way life-threatening. The doctor had told him not to expect much of the hair to grow back, but not to worry about the wound itself.

The morning after Drayton sailed, he chartered a boat back to Dunkirk. There he stole the first available motorcycle and rode back along the road to the big British encampment.

RETURN TO THE FRONT

When Ledyard walked through the double doors of the shell-shock ward the first person he saw was Reston.

"Well, there you are," the orderly exclaimed. "The Yanks have been looking high and low for you."

After a few minutes the mustached doctor and two British soldiers appeared.

"I would say you've healed up quite well," the doctor said, running his eyes over the scalp wound. "Where have you been?"

"Out, I guess," Ledyard answered, playing dumb.

"Well," the doctor said, rising to his feet, "the Americans are anxious to see you. Good luck."

The stoic escort ushered him outside. There they climbed into a waiting car and, after a drive of several hours, arrived at the American bivouac.

They pulled up in front of a building surrounded with tall rolls of barbed wire, and at the gated entrance Ledyard was handed over to a pair of American guards.

Taking his arms as if they were guiding an old woman across the street, the guards walked him into a room, ordered him to sit in a chair and told him to wait.

Ten minutes later two American officers came into the room, pulled chairs close to him and sat down. One was lean and carried a manila file. The other was small eyed and chunky. Neither one introduced themselves.

"Alright soldier," the man with the file started, "we're not here to bullshit you . . ."

"So don't bullshit us," the chunky officer said, finishing the sentence. They asked his name, rank and the unit he had been attached to. The officer with the file leaned in close. "You were in an attack on the eleventh, is that right?"

"I don't remember the day," Ledyard answered, "but I remember what happened."

"Tell us about it?" said the chunky officer.

"It's a long story."

His interrogators smiled at each other and the officer with the file leaned forward again. "Our time is your time, son."

Ledyard gave them a factual chronology of what had happened to him. He left out the French woman, telling them that he had hidden in the barn of an abandoned estate until the arrival of the Germans forced him to flee again. He told them about his dash through the gas and flying through the air when the shell hit behind him. The officers listened expressionless to his story, speaking only when they wanted him to continue.

"That's about it," he said.

"Did you have any intercourse with the enemy?"

"Only with the fellow at the cistern, the one with the motorcycle."

"No one else?"

"Why would I?" Ledyard asked.

"Just answer the question."

"The answer is no." Ledyard looked at them in disbelief. "You think I went over?" he asked. The interrogators didn't answer, and Ledyard snickered. "You think I'm some kind of spy." His two interrogators looked so pitiful in their seriousness that Ledyard burst out laughing but the questioners did not see the humor in it.

"Where have you been since you walked away from the hospital?" the chunky one asked.

Ledyard's surprise and disbelief turned to loathing. They were focusing their energy on him instead of the mountains of dead and wounded on the battlefield.

"They are the war," he thought.

"Where have you been since you left the hospital?"

"Why don't you tell me?" Ledyard asked.

"You just answer the question, soldier," growled the man with the file.

"I . . . don't . . . know."

The chunky officer had folded his arms across his chest. "You're saying you were . . ."

"I remember walking and eating and drinking but I don't know what I was doing," Ledyard interrupted.

"What did you do with the horse?"

"What horse?" The man with the file was thumbing it unconsciously.

"The horse you walked away with. The horse you were asking about. It was the same one wasn't it?"

"I took him to England and shipped him back to New York." The interview stretched deep into the afternoon. Ledyard played his whole life as spotty remembrances in a fog of contradiction and hoped that the random, insistent pattern of his lying would force them to conclude that a powerful knock on the head really had scrambled his brain.

It was a dangerous game.

If his act had broken down or if they had caught him in obvious lies he would have been in deep water. If he had irritated them enough, a trumped-up case might have been brought against him. Anything could have happened.

The lean man with the file suggested they begin again with the story of his lost days behind the lines and Ledyard played along, reiterating it all once more. This time the interrogators interrupted with many questions but Ledyard was ready for them.

"Was there more than one German at this cistern?"

Ledyard dropped his eyes to the floor and thought for a few seconds. "You think so?"

"We weren't there soldier."

"Maybe there were others hiding under the vines," Ledyard offered.

"Did you see any other Germans at the cistern?"

"No . . . but that doesn't mean they weren't there. I know I saw one, that's for sure."

The interview continued in the same vein. He answered most of their questions with confusing ones of his own. And when he described events, he did so with as much poetic flair as possible.

The story of his crossing the German lines was particularly well done and when he finished the two officers were sitting on the edge of their chairs in rapt attention.

Ledyard broke the silence by asking, "Is that horse dead? He sure was a good jumper."

The interview ended there, and Ledyard was escorted to an open stockade where he spent the night with a half-dozen criminals the army had detained.

After breakfast the same men interviewed him again. This session lasted until nearly noon and frayed everyone's nerves.

Ledyard grew so weary of the repetition that he thought at one point "I should ask for a lawyer." But in the same instant he knew he shouldn't. A lawyer would draw even greater attention and the army, in the midst of helping prosecute a world war, would be provoked.

The questioning ended inconclusively and his tormentors left, never to return.

Ledyard remained in the stockade for more than a week.

During that time he was shown dozens of pictures of men he had never seen but was asked if he knew. Living men, some in uniform, some out, came to the stockade fence and looked at him. A smiling chaplain visited him twice asking all sorts of questions but nothing about why he was there. A woman in a black dress came to the fence and broke down in tears. One afternoon a horse was brought to the fence by two officers who carefully watched the animal's face in case there was a reaction. Who the horse was, the woman, the pictures; all of it was a complete mystery to Ledyard.

On his last morning a man who Ledyard recognized came to the fence. It was a boy he had been with in the forward observation trench. His name was Bill Teagarden and he looked much older than he had on the day of the attack.

Bill narrowed his eyes.

"Is that you Ledyard?"

"Bill Teagarden?"

"Right." A ghostly smile flitted across Bill's mouth. "What they got you in here for?"

"I guess that's what I'd like to know."

"Alright," an officer interjected. "Is he or isn't he?"

"Yeah," said Teagarden, "that's Ledyard Dixon." Bill's identification proved nothing except that he could identify a fellow-soldier, but it provided the army with the only excuse it needed to rid itself of a silly problem, and Ledyard was released that afternoon. He was issued new clothing and gear, given a bunk in the barracks and told to report to personnel the first thing next morning for reassignment.

Ledyard's release was prompted by a recent sharp rise in American casualties. The top brass had sent down a directive to medical units and investigative services that anyone fit for duty should be back on duty. Fearing wrath from on high, the hospitals disgorged borderline cases, and stockades emptied off all but the most heinous criminals.

Ledyard got back into the war.

He was ordered to another reconnaissance unit, and two days later found himself once again in a forward observation trench awaiting the commencement of an artillery barrage. As usual, the barrage would signal the beginning of a countdown, which, once complete, would send him over the top.

Ledyard prepared in the same way he and the dead boy from Montana had prepared prior to their first attack. While he steeled himself against the trench wall absorbing the shock of constant explosions, he tried to think good thoughts. He tried to think of Drayton as a whistle sounded and he scrambled up to face the enemy.

German artillery was falling as he and the other clench-jawed fighters dashed across no-man's land. One of the blasts knocked him off his feet and he lay still making sure he was not hit before he got up to run.

But as he got up Ledyard happened to look into the mouth of a crater and was astounded to see a young man in uniform, his arms hugging his legs, his head against his knees, rocking back and forth like a child against the wall of the hole. Everything was the same, the bodies, the pool of water at the bottom, the rain which had begun to fall. Ledyard thought he was hallucinating. He was certain that the man would turn his head at any moment and the face would be his own.

The head of the soldier did begin to turn and as Ledyard watched dumbstruck from the lip of the crater a mournful face he had never seen before stared up at him from the hole.

Ledyard never heard the explosion. It blew him off his feet and into the crater. He landed near the bottom and lay still, too shocked to feel or move. Suddenly, he was aware of someone and saw the man with the mournful face creeping toward him. He was taking his jacket off as he splashed through the water. His eyes were focused low on Ledyard's body.

Ledyard's gaze traveled down his left leg until it ended just below the knee. There was only blood, and it was pouring out of him.

HOME

Ledyard lost his leg sixteen days before the German surrender.

The surgeon who originally tied off his veins and arteries did such a poor job that the recovery was fraught with setbacks. The wound ruptured several times, necessitating more surgeries, and the temporary wooden prosthesis he had received spent weeks standing against the wall behind his bed.

The first letter he got had come from his father. The hastily penned note was short but they were the happiest words he ever read. "Drayton and I arrived in Grand Rapids on the twelfth. Both in good health. Love, Dad."

Ledyard kept the note as a talisman and was still carrying it when his train pulled into the Grand Rapids station on the day before Christmas, 1918.

The whole family and a number of friends had ventured into bitter cold to meet him. Drayton was there too, cloaked in a heavy blanket, standing on the platform near the head of the train.

When all the passengers had detrained and Ledyard had still not appeared, the welcoming party waited as his father and his Uncle Cecil boarded the train to look for him.

Ledyard had been in the last car and had to wait while a conductor located his misplaced duffel bag. Once that was found it took him a little extra time to disembark, owing to the lack of practice he'd had walking on wood.

As the family huddled at one end of the platform Ledyard shouldered the big bag and started toward them from the other end, quickly settling into the distinctive swinging gate of a man on a stump.

When he was halfway down the platform someone spotted him, and a collective gasp of shock emanated from the small group of greeters. They all knew what had happened to him, but no amount of foreknowledge could have prepared them for the sight of the grim man walking toward them. How could this be their Ledyard?

His mother was hardest hit at the vision of her golden boy reduced to wreckage. She cried out, her hand going to her mouth. But the shock of seeing him quickly gave way to a frenzy of shouting, embracing and kissing. He had been reduced, but the fact that he was still alive was cause for celebration.

Ledyard turned this way and that in the throng without giving anyone his full attention. It had been aimed at the disabled horse. When he could stand it no longer, Ledyard burst free of their grasps, gave his father a half embrace, threw himself around Drayton's neck and began to cry.

While Ledyard wept, the family and well wishers stood to one side. All of them felt awkward in the role of involuntary voyeurs. None of them had to know the details of what had transpired between man and animal. The anguish and joy and love running down Ledyard's face as he held the horse told all that really needed to be known.

When he had vented himself Ledyard began to look Drayton over and, as he did, the family and friends came back to life, pressing toward him with the questions and salutations that are common to all homecomings.

But Ledyard never did come home.

It was clear to him from the start that he could not stay in Michigan. After what he had experienced, home was too familiar. Main Street, the snow, the faces of people he had known from childhood, his favorite boyhood haunts, the destiny of the town and even the house he grew up in was somehow devoid of life.

He shared these feelings with no one, but his father could tell that Ledyard was different. A week after the arrival, he and his son sat down for a private talk in the study.

The house was empty for the first time since his return, and they said nothing as they stared at the lively, yellow flames of the fire.

"Mother's devastated, isn't she?" Ledyard said, breaking the silence.

"I hope you don't think she's rejecting you."

"Oh, I don't think that, Father. I think she just loves me too much to see me like this."

His father knew it was true. A pocket of gas hissed and sizzled in one of the logs and the men waited until it ceased.

"I can't stay here, Father."

The elder Dixon brought one of his hands up and began to stroke his forehead.

"I've been feeling that," he said. "But . . . uhhh . . . you should know that there is no way that I or your mother . . . could actively encourage you to leave. We would be so happy to have you here."

"But I wouldn't."

"No, no. I can see that." Ledyard's father was ready to break down. "Let me have one of your cigarettes will you?" Ledyard smiled in wonder at his father.

"You don't smoke, Dad."

"Well, give me one anyway." Ledyard shook one out of the pack, lit it and handed it across. His father held it up toward the light of the fire, stuck it in his mouth and puffed like the beginner he was.

"Not bad," he said, eyeing the cigarette between his fingers. Ledyard laughed and there was silence again. His father seemed nervous. He puffed at the cigarette, leaned forward to flick the ashes into the fire and settled back to puff some more. At last he brought himself to ask what he yearned to know.

"I would sure like to know what happened to you son."

"I wouldn't mind telling you, Father. I would like to tell somebody something. but I can't begin to think how to start."

"Start anywhere you want. Start with Drayton. Tell me what you like about him . . . anything."

And that is how Ledyard began, talking about the animal he had found on the battlefield. The rest came out easily.

He told about his abortive first attack, his close calls and the strange encounters he'd experienced in his wanderings.

His father listened to the chronology of events attentively, sometimes wincing at the privations his son had endured.

Talking about the French woman was hard. Though he revealed none of the details of their passion, his halting descriptions of her needed no embellishment. It was obvious he had been in love.

It was impossible to talk about what had happened to her without breaking down and Ledyard struggled not to. He turned his face to the fire, trying to quash the lump in his throat.

When he looked back tears were streaming down his father's face and his voice quavered as he spoke.

"She's dead, isn't she?" Ledyard's eyes dropped. He nodded. A little wail of sorrow escaped his father's mouth. He caught his head with a hand as it pitched forward.

"My poor son," he whispered, "my poor, poor son."

Ledyard had never seen his father cry, and he had never imagined that there would ever be a time when they would cry together. But they did on that winter afternoon in the study.

For several minutes each sat in their chairs crying out a father and a son's mutual grief in front of a cheery fire.

As his sobbing trailed away Ledyard's father ran a shirtsleeve across his face and said, "I don't think I can hear anymore right now."

"That's alright father."

"I want to hear all that you're willing to share, but I can't just now." Ledyard said nothing. His father threw his head back against the chair and, still sniffling said, "Maybe we should just go down and visit Drayton for awhile." They were often with Drayton that winter, hanging around his stall or taking him for walks in the snow, and they became close in ways that fathers and sons rarely do.

The elder Dixon became Ledyard's protector. He was the only one who knew how thoroughly his son's life had been ruined and how much the crippled horse meant to him. He understood the detachment in Ledyard, and he didn't push his one-legged boy. Nor did he ever let his sorrow show again. He let him be.

The space his father provided was a wonderful boon for Ledyard. He did not have to explain the hours spent in his room, nor was there a fuss when he excused himself from most social activities. And when it was whispered that the amount of time Ledyard spent with Drayton might be unhealthy for a young veteran with so much to live for, his father rose up like a lion and smashed such talk.

When he wasn't with Drayton, Ledyard could be found in his Uncle Cecil's painting studio. There he was schooled in the basics of handling brushes and applying color, and before January was out they were painting together regularly.

Despite the companionship of Drayton, his father's protection and his uncle's tutoring, Ledyard's days passed too slowly. He itched to break away from the suffocation of the past, and when the weather broke toward the end of March he and Drayton boarded a train west to a town called Santa Barbara, which Uncle Cecil had recommended.

His father went to great lengths to ensure that the departure would be free of dramatics. When it was time to embrace his son he looked into Ledyard's eyes and said firmly, "I want an address as soon as you've got one."

The gloom that descended on Ledyard's family after he was gone stayed in varying degrees for the rest of their lives. The son who went to California was not going to come back, and his mother often despaired at having lost him.

There wasn't much her husband could do to reassure her, because he felt much the same himself.

He did point out the son they missed had never really come back to them. The boy who had stayed with them through the winter was more a lodger than a son. The war had taken him like it had so many thousands of others. The best they could do was pray that he would find peace.

But nothing he could say ever altered the fact that their lives were destined to be played out with an integral part missing.

INTO THE STARS

Ledyard never made it to California. As mile after mile clicked past, he fretted about where he might end up.

He wanted to be far from the taint of human endeavor – the corruption of politics, the greed of economics, the waste of war – and wasn't sure California was the place.

He had never been there, but he had heard wonderful things, talk of opportunity, easy living and glamour. These wonderful attributes bothered him.

When the train stopped in a small Northern New Mexico town, he got off to water Drayton and realized he had what he wanted.

Within two weeks a local real estate agent had located a crumbling adobe house that nobody wanted. It was set back from a big river in a grove of old cottonwoods. The property bordered a great tract of government land, and Ledyard bought the place the same day he saw it.

He and Drayton spent the first month on the property without having a single visitor. The only contact Ledyard had with anyone was on weekly trips to town for groceries, and then he spoke only when spoken to.

The rest of the time he spent dreaming about painting

and what to do with the place.

He thought incessantly about how to proceed with his life and decided at last that the key lay in changing his outlook. His life might have been wrecked, but by what standard? He knew that no satisfaction could come if he compared his one leg against everyone else's two.

There was no way he could continue to live by the duplicitous standards that had marched him to Europe and carried him back out. The only way he could visualize getting anything from the years that lay before him was to reject the world as he had known it and create his own.

The first thing he did was hire a crew of half a dozen Mexican men to refurbish the adobe house. One of them was a graying, grizzled man named Francisco Robles who had ideas.

One afternoon when the work was nearly finished, Ledyard was standing in the big room contemplating an easel when he saw Francisco looking in from the doorway.

"I've been thinking, Señor Dixon."

"I'm sure you have, Francisco." Francisco waved a hand at the tangle of paint and brushes and canvas in the room.

"A painter should have a studio."

Ledyard glanced at him thoughtfully. He had wondered about a studio but kept going back and forth.

Francisco scratched his head. "I could build you one," he said.

The studio took a long time to build because Francisco did most of it by himself. With or without helpers he came every day, and in the time it took to erect Ledyard's creative retreat the two men established a rhythm between them that became a partnership.

This was largely because Francisco comprehended Ledyard. A man with one leg and a side of his scalp sheared off must have experienced terrible pain. There must be suffering inside as well. No one could know the depth of another man's trials, and there was no point inquiring into something that was inexplicable.

The one thing Francisco knew for sure was that the crippled horse and the crippled man had something extraordinary between them. What it was held no interest for Francisco. He could see that they loved each other and that was all he needed to know.

In a few weeks' time, Francisco had settled so deeply into the life of the place that anyone passing through would have little trouble believing he had been born on the same piece of land.

Weeks stretched into months until one morning Francisco knocked at the door of the studio with his hat in hand. His face looked melancholy.

"I can't see anymore to do," he said plaintively.

"I'm sure we can find something," Ledyard said, dropping what he had been doing.

"I don't want you to make work for me Señor Dixon."

Ledyard was panicking. There must be something for the Mexican to do that wouldn't kill his pride.

Francisco's eyes narrowed. "I could build a barn."

"A barn? Drayton doesn't need a barn."

"It would be Drayton and some others."

"Other horses?"

"Yes. Horses like the company of their own kind." Ledyard didn't like the idea.

"I'll have to think about it Francisco," he said. Ledyard did not have to think very long. He knew almost from the time the door shut that Francisco was right. He called the worker back and the two spent the rest of the day searching out the right piece of ground on which to place the barn.

As they sketched out various ideas in the dirt, Francisco had another idea. "I was thinking Señor Dixon . . ."

"Uhhh-huh . . ."

"I was thinking . . . if I take care of these horses."

"Not Drayton."

"No, no the others . . . it might be good if I had a place . . . to take a siesta . . . make some coffee."

The barn was completed around the anniversary of Ledyard and Drayton's arrival in New Mexico, and soon three horses were led into new stalls. They, too, had been marked for rendering, and their happiness at having a home was palpable.

Francisco had moved into the barn long before it was finished. Both he and Ledyard knew by that time that he was staying for life, but they never spoke of it.

Ledyard painted everything. His work was difficult because he put all of himself into it. Over time he developed an edgy style that lent a kinetic quality to his canvases. He never penetrated the pricy eastern markets, but that did not trouble him. There was a steady enough demand for his pictures in the west, and after a few years he was earning a good living.

Once in a great while he would make a painting of the war. They were ferocious and he worked them out fast, attacking the canvas with the same uncompromising strength that was embodied in the images. Even he did not know precisely why he was driven to do them.

Ledyard lived inside himself but was not hermit-like. The country was full of painters, and over the years he met most of them. One or two became more than passing acquaintances.

It was the same with all of his friendships. He kept his life, and especially his past, to himself.

From time to time he longed for women. A few made him ache, but he was careful not to cross the threshold that held him back. He did not know exactly what the threshold was made of and often he wished it didn't exist, but he always went home alone.

Ledyard never back-pedaled on his beliefs. He immersed himself in the moment and in beauty and succeeded in serving them both. He pursued these beliefs in the pictures he made, the people he met, the books he read and the place he lived. He surrendered to the drama of the natural world around him. He woke when he was rested, ate when he was hungry and slept when he was tired. He possessed neither a clock or a telephone and never regretted their absence.

As the years folded one into another, Drayton became the epitome of what Ledyard was living for. They were always together, walking in the aspen groves along the river or across the long mesa that loomed above. When the weather was calm and agreeable, Ledyard would roll up a few blankets and they would pass the night in the open as they had when they first met.

The act of living was something they did in tandem, and the unity they shared was such that no one who came near them could fail to notice it.

Francisco said it best one afternoon after he had watched their slow return from an outing at the river.

"That Drayton . . . he lives for you. And you live for him."

The words were true. The peace they found together was impregnable. It was a wall that kept the war and all its agonies at bay.

But war could never be vanquished entirely. Its infidelity was something each of them carried on their bodies.

Ledyard's circulation pestered him off and on. Sometimes his leg would swell and it was hard for him to get around. And there were times when pain shot through his head so violently that his eyes would water.

Drayton's wound bothered him too. His limp had wild fluctuations. Some days he moved with only a hint of his disability while on others he could barely walk. Occasionally, he remained all day in his stall dozing the hours away.

And there was the coughing. Both of them came back from Europe with a persistent cough that grew worse, especially when temperatures soared or plummeted.

The veterinarian attributed Drayton's affliction to "weak lungs" but could recommend no antidote.

Ledyard put off seeing a doctor, and when he finally went, the general practitioner listened to his lungs for a long time, his stethoscope searching out every nuance of Ledyard's breathing. When he finally pulled the plugs from his ears he grunted to himself and looked squarely at his patient.

"You were in the Great War?"

"Yes."

"Were you ever gassed?"

"Not severely."

The doctor grunted to himself again.

"Well, we don't know much about that damned

gas, but the effects seem to depend pretty much on the individual."

"What about me?" Ledyard asked.

"Don't know for sure. But there's definitely something wrong. I'd say your lungs are degenerating."

"Is this something that's going to kill me?"

"Professionally, I couldn't say for sure."

"Personally?"

"Probably," the doctor said.

Ledyard didn't really need the doctor's opinion. He knew he was going downhill. So was Drayton.

Francisco knew it too. The range of Ledyard and Drayton's outings diminished until they no longer went to the river or climbed onto the mesa. Even Ledyard's trips to the barn were taxing, and at last he began to ask Francisco to bring Drayton up. The walk from the house to the studio began to drain him, and when Ledyard took to spending some days in bed, Francisco knew he was dying.

He saw the same thing happen in the barn. Drayton's listlessness deepened and Francisco noticed that the horse's breathing sounded more and more labored even though he was standing still.

The onset of winter only made their conditions graver. Ledyard wrote a long letter to his parents. He had Francisco ship the war paintings to his father.

He did not mind dying. In fact, he would have looked forward to taking his place with the multitudes who had gone before him had it not been for Drayton. He could not bear to think of leaving him behind.

He thought of spending his last days in the barn, but rejected the idea because the emotion would be too great for both of them. So he stayed put in the bedroom, reading when he had the strength, watching the fire Francisco kept stoked and dreaming when he closed his eyes.

The dreams were more vivid than he ever thought possible. The French woman was often there, but he did not see her as the object of desire she had once been. She came to him now as a face or a pair of eyes, a full mouth with shining teeth, a head of luxuriant hair brought to life by the breeze. She was always looking at him, the mischievous light of love alive in her eyes.

On the night he died, the dream that had recurred so often came to him once more. The dream seemed grander than it had ever been. He and Drayton in glorious triumph, plowing through space toward the inevitable rendezvous with the stars.

When he woke, he saw Francisco squatting in front of the fireplace turning logs.

Ledyard sucked air into his wasted lungs. It gave him little relief, but he continued to struggle. He wanted so badly to see Drayton, to touch him, to smell him, to tell him how much he loved him.

Francisco pulled a chair close to the bed and sat down. His face was long and sad. He dropped his eyes and toyed with the brim of his hat.

"Say something," Ledyard wheezed.

Francisco sighed in anguish. His eyes were swimming with wetness. "It's very hard to say, Señor."

"Talk," Ledyard commanded feebly.

"Drayton is down. I don't think he will get up."

"Is he comfortable?" Ledyard whispered.

"I put extra hay all around him, Señor." Francisco brushed away the tears that stood ready to fall down his face, and when he looked again at Ledyard he could see that a great calm had descended on him.

"Comfortable?" Francisco asked.

Ledyard nodded. "Let me sleep," he whispered, closing his eyes for the last time.

Bundled against the cold, Francisco trudged back to the barn. Drayton lay in perfect peace, his flanks no longer heaving.

Francisco ran back to the house and found that Ledyard too had stopped breathing.

The Mexican stepped outside. He needed the night air in his lungs. He needed it on his face. His usually clear mind was crowded with emotions he could not handle, and not knowing what else to do he lifted his eyes to the stars.

They hung in the heavens as though they had just been born, and as Francisco stood staring at the necklaces of light crossing the sky, it came to him.

Ledyard and Drayton had passed out of the world together. It could never have been any other way.

About ZOVA Books

Vision

ZOVA Books delivers quality works of fiction by established authors. Our team is committed to publishing books using the highest quality printing methods with the best printing products. ZOVA Books has a firm foundation in the art of book printing while seeking and embracing the future of digital publishing.

Mission

ZOVA Books is an independent publishing company serving discriminating readers and booksellers of quality. We strive to create dynamic and successful partnerships for our authors, vendors, and retailers. ZOVA Books seeks to build the next generation publishing firm.

Visit us at zovabooks.com

ZOVA **BOOKS**
LOS ANGELES

zovabooks.com
zovabooks.blogspot.com
facebook.com/ZOVAbooks
twitter.com/ZOVAbooks